come the morning

with love,

Maria

LANDSCAPES OF CHILDHOOD

come

the

morning

Mark Jonathan Harris

Photographs by Marissa Roth

New Edition with Author's Commentary

Wayne State University Press Detroit

New edition published 2005 by Wayne State University Press, Detroit, MI 48201. Originally published by Bradbury Press. No part of this book may be reproduced without formal permission. Manufactured in the United States of America.
09 08 07 06 05   1 2 3 4 5

Library of Congress Cataloging-in-Publication Data

Harris, Mark Jonathan, 1941-
   Come the morning / Mark Jonathan Harris ; photographs by Marissa Roth.— New ed. with author's commentary.
       p. cm. — (Landscapes of childhood)
   ISBN 0-8143-3241-2 (pbk. : alk. paper)
   1. Los Angeles (Calif.)—Fiction. 2. Fatherless families—Fiction.
   3. Homeless teenagers—Fiction. 4. Poor families—Fiction.
   5. Teenage boys—Fiction. I. Title. II. Series.
   PS3558.A64815C66 2005
   813'.54—dc22   2004019245

∞The paper used in this publication meets the minimum require-ments of the American National Standard for Information Sciences—Permanence of Paper for Printed Library Materials, ANSI Z39.48-1984.

For Susan

1

Ben Gibson awoke to find the city rising before him like a fortress. The glass and steel towers shimmered in the early morning light, bouncing the sun from one silvered window to another.

"A city of dreams," his father had called it.

Even in the Monday morning traffic, the Greyhound bus was moving too quickly for Ben to take everything in. The buildings whirled past him at a dizzying speed. Their height, the boldness of their shapes, took his breath away.

Excitedly he nudged Felice. "Wake up! We're here."

His sister stirred groggily, groped for her pink-haired doll. Ben pressed his face back up against the dirty window. The bus shifted lanes and moved toward an exit on the freeway.

Felice squeezed beside him at the window. "Where's the ocean?" she asked. "I don't see the ocean."

" 'Cause it's not there," he said sharply. For almost

the whole twenty-hour trip from El Paso, she'd been griping about one thing or another.

Felice turned to their mother, reading her Bible in the seat across the aisle. "You said there was a beach," she complained.

"Hush," Constance warned, both to silence her and to keep from waking Jube, who lay sleeping on his mother's lap. At three he was the baby of the family— six years younger than Felice and ten younger than Ben—and Constance was always fretting over him.

Felice raised her doll to the window as the bus pulled off the freeway into downtown Los Angeles. "What do you think, Millie?" She pushed the doll's plastic face against the glass. "She says it's just a big, ugly city," Felice muttered loud enough for Constance to hear.

"Millie's blind," Ben retorted. He found the city as dazzling as his father had described, as full of wealth and promise. The streets were crowded with well-dressed people hurrying to their offices, men with dark suits and leather briefcases, women in high heels and colored stockings. "It's a place where anybody can strike it rich," his father had often said about L.A., although nothing like that had happened to Clyde Gibson the few months he'd lived there. Still, Ben thought, the people who named the streets must have seen the city in the same way. Hope Street. Grand Street. Spring Street. "They named it the city of angels for the angels who watch over your dreams." Whenever his father talked about Los Angeles, Ben sensed that he regretted not staying there long enough for the angels to hear his own dreams.

Clyde Gibson had worked in L.A. for a brief time as a

mechanic when he'd gotten out of the army. Then Clyde's father became sick and Clyde went home to El Paso to help out his mother. The week after Clyde's father died, he met Constance at the hardware store where she was clerking and decided to stay in Texas for a while. A few months later they were married and in another year Ben was born. The first few years of Ben's life, his father worked the oil fields, but then he injured his back in a fall from a derrick and took a less strenuous job at an auto parts factory. Although he sometimes talked about moving to California to make better money, Constance always had the same reply: "Why go all that way for a few more dollars when we're doing just fine here?"

Then, out of the blue, a year and a half ago, the factory that employed Ben's father shut down. Though Clyde looked hard for work, jobs in west Texas were suddenly as scarce as rain. After several months Constance had to leave Jube at home with Clyde and go to work herself waiting tables at a coffee shop to make ends meet. More and more discouraged, Clyde finally gave up even hunting for a job. One Saturday morning, five months ago in September, Ben stumbled into the kitchen for breakfast to find his mother in tears. Sometime during the night, his father had driven away in his Pontiac.

As the bus moved farther downtown, Ben noticed the buildings and people begin to change. The sky-scrapers gave way to doughnut and record shops. The men on the streets carried bedrolls and knapsacks, and the women were plain and tired-looking like his mother. There were many more brown and black faces now and no one looked like a movie star. In fact, this part of the city was even poorer and shabbier than the Gibsons' last neighborhood in El Paso.

"Yecch! Look how dirty it is," Felice said in disgust, pointing to an alley littered with garbage.

Ben glanced over at his mother to see if she had noticed, too, but she was looking out the other window and he couldn't see her expression.

Jube awoke as the bus turned into the Greyhound station. "Is this it? Are we here?" he asked sleepily.

"Welcome to Los Angeles," Felice read aloud the greeting brightly stenciled on the cement wall at the station entrance. Just beneath it someone had spray-painted in red a single comment: "Ha!"

The driver stood outside the bus door saying good-bye to his passengers as they exited. "Good luck," he added when Constance stepped down holding Jube's hand. Ben wondered if everyone could tell just by look-ing at them how down on their luck they'd been.

He helped his mother retrieve their two, worn plaid suitcases from the baggage compartment beneath the bus. Constance had stuffed as many of their belongings into them as she could and they were as heavy as stones. Ben was small for his age, and slender like his mother, and he could barely carry a bag ten yards before he had to put it down and change hands. But by tugging and sliding as much as lifting, he and his mother managed to get their frayed luggage to the esca-lator and down to the ground floor of the station.

They stopped by the lockers to catch their breath. From her Bible, Constance removed the envelope Clyde Gibson had sent her a week before. It was the

4

first—and only—message from him since he'd disappeared with his car. Never easy with words, Clyde had grown even more silent after he lost his job, and left only the barest note when he vanished from El Paso: "I don't want to drag you down any more. You'll be better off without me." The envelope he mailed them from Los Angeles had nothing more to add. All that it contained was a $100 money order posted in his name. Still, it confirmed what Ben and his mother faithfully believed, that Clyde would send for them as soon as he got back on his feet again.

Constance looked again at the return address printed in delicate gray type on the back of the fancy envelope. The stationery was as mysterious as the unexpected money order. Was the address a boardinghouse where Clyde was living? A place where he was employed? Constance hadn't been able to find the answer by telephone. The Los Angeles operator had no number listed in Clyde's name. Still, Ben and Constance had both agreed Clyde wouldn't have sent a return address unless he wanted them to be able to find him.

"Do you think it's far from here?" Ben asked.

"We got to find out," Constance said. "But first we need to freshen up." She stood guard over their suitcases while Ben led Jube to the men's room. When they returned, Constance took her purse and shopping bag and went off to the ladies' room with Felice.

A few minutes later she returned in a blue flowered dress, her Sunday best. The change from jeans to church clothes made Ben realize just how nervous she was about seeing his father again.

A row of taxis waited outside the station. Constance

showed the envelope to the first driver in line, a large man with slicked hair, a thin mustache, and a belly that spilled over his sagging trousers. He looked at the address and then back to Constance as if they didn't quite match.

"Cost you about thirty-five dollars from here," he said, handing the envelope back.

"That much?" Constance's face crimped with worry. The fare was almost half the price of a bus ticket from El Paso to Los Angeles. "Is there another way to get there?" she asked.

"That's up in the hills, lady, in Bel-Air. It'll take you two buses to get even close, but you'll still need a taxi to get the rest of the way." The driver leaned against his blue and gold Celebrity Cab and twirled his spiky mustache while he waited for Ben's mother to make up her mind.

Constance looked down at their heavy suitcases. "Maybe we should check these in the lockers and take the bus."

"We're only going to have to come back for them again," Ben said, impatient with her caution.

"You're right," she said. "If we're going to have to take a taxi anyway, might as well ride all the way. . . ." She nodded to the driver, and he shuffled over to their suitcases and lifted them as easily as if they'd been empty.

The Gibsons piled into the back of the taxi and the cabbie eased his huge belly underneath the steering wheel. He flipped on the meter and they pulled away.

In a few minutes the taxi was speeding down the freeway, heading west from downtown. The soaring office buildings gave way to flat stretches of tiled-roof houses dotted with asparaguslike palm trees. The city seemed to stretch for miles on either side of the freeway.

"I bet Daddy will be pretty surprised to see us," Felice said.

"I expect so," Constance said, anxiously watching the meter.

"Do you think he can take us to Disneyland tomorrow?" Felice babbled on. As usual, Ben thought, she's thinking only about what she wants. From his mother's drawn face, he guessed that she was worrying about how his father would react to their sudden appearance.

The decision to follow Clyde to Los Angeles had not been an easy one for her. His father's abrupt departure had left her shaken and uncertain. She'd had to give up waitressing during the day to stay home with Jube and had taken a job cleaning office buildings at night. They had almost no El Paso relatives to turn to—both Constance's and Clyde's parents were dead—and the few cousins in town looked down on them because they were so poor. Ben had tried to help out as much as he could, delivering handbills after school for extra money and taking care of his brother and sister when Constance worked at night. Yet, even with his help, they still had trouble breaking even.

When the money arrived from his father, Ben urged his mother to spend it on bus fare to L.A. What was there to stay for in El Paso? They didn't like the neighborhood where they'd been forced to move. His mother had no prospects for a better job, and soon they might have to move to an even worse neighborhood.

Still, his mother worried about making such a bold move, about giving up her job and their apartment, taking Ben and Felice out of school. . . . What if Clyde wasn't ready for them yet? For several days she prayed for guidance before finally making up her mind: Despite the uncertainties, they would be better off selling their broken-down furniture and reuniting with Clyde in California.

At $20.25 the driver turned north onto another freeway. Constance leaned forward a little to get a better view of the meter. "We got far to go?" she asked the driver.

"About ten more dollars' worth," he answered.

Three dollars later the cab turned off the freeway onto Sunset Boulevard. At the first corner a boy about the same age as Ben, who probably should have been in school, sat in a folding chair beside a large, hand-painted wooden sign advertising "Star Maps."

"Look!" Felice pointed. "Do movie stars live around here?"

"*Si*, up and down these hills," the driver said as if they were as common as the gardeners watering the lush lawns.

Ben, however, was impressed. The homes were stone and brick mansions and Spanish haciendas, with bright beds of spring flowers, and shiny sports cars parked in their driveways. He couldn't imagine anyone but movie stars living in houses that splendid.

The cabbie drove another mile or so down Sunset then passed through the imposing, cement and steel archway of the west gate of Bel-Air. The road narrowed to two lanes and wound its way upward into the hills past even larger estates, shrouded by trees and dense shrubbery and protected by wrought iron or thick wooden gates. Behind the stone walls and thick foliage Ben glimpsed tennis courts and terraced swimming pools.

The driver slowed the cab and turned into a macadam driveway. "Here you are," he said. The iron gate was open and the cabbie pulled up in front of a gabled, two-story, white brick house that was four or five times as big as the bungalow they'd rented before Ben's father lost his job.

"Is this where Daddy lives?" Felice asked. It was grander than Ben had even dared to hope.

"Nine forty Stradella, that's the address you gave me," the driver said, turning off the meter.

Constance checked the envelope in her Bible to be sure. This was hardly the boardinghouse she had expected. But there was no mistake. It was the same address. She took out her wallet and paid the driver $35. The fare was $33.50 and she let him keep the change for a tip.

Opening the taxi door, she looked up again at the magnificent white house and hesitated. "Maybe you'd better wait a minute before you unload the suitcases," she told the driver.

"Whatever you say, lady."

"You'd better wait, too, and mind your brother and sister," she told Ben as she stepped out of the cab.

"I don't want to stay. I want to see my daddy," Jube said, following her out the door. Felice was right behind him and then Ben. He hadn't come all this way to wait now, either.

Seeing the three of them standing beside the cab, Constance decided not to argue. They trailed a few steps behind her as she walked to the front of the house and rang the bell.

A small brown-skinned woman answered the door with a feather duster in her hand. Constance asked for Clyde Gibson.

The woman looked puzzled. Constance repeated his name.

"No here," the woman said.

"Is he out?" Constance asked.

The woman didn't seem to understand. "No live here," she said, starting to close the door.

"Wait! Please . . ." Constance stopped her.

"Okay. I get missus," the cleaning woman said.

Ben looked nervously at his mother. There were tiny beads of perspiration on her forehead.

A moment later a tall woman appeared in the doorway in high heels and a long skirt, both arms jangling with gold and silver bracelets. Ben was glad his mother had changed to her best dress.

"Is there something I can do for you?" the woman asked. Her eyes swept over the four of them to the cab in the driveway.

"I'm looking for my husband . . . Clyde Gibson. . . ." Constance's voice faltered.

The woman looked mystified. "I'm afraid you must have the wrong address. I don't know anyone by that name."

Constance's face went gray as lead. She reached into her coat pocket and pulled out the envelope.

"That's my stationery all right," the woman said, puzzled. "How did you get it?"

"My husband sent it to me. Last week. Wait, I'll show you his picture." Constance opened her wallet

10

with a shaking hand and showed the woman a photograph of the two of them with their arms around each other, taken before all their troubles began.

The woman examined the picture a moment. "His face does look familiar. . . . Of course! He worked here a couple of weeks ago. Clearing the brush in the back. When I paid him, I must have put the money in one of my envelopes." She seemed pleased to have remembered.

"Do you know where I can find him now?" Constance asked.

"I'm sorry, but I have no idea," the woman said.

"Didn't he leave any address?" Ben asked.

Constance reached down and squeezed his hand, whether to quiet him or to steady herself he didn't know.

"Well, you see he just worked here for the day," the woman explained. "My gardener picked him up at one of those day-labor agencies downtown. I'm not even sure what the name of it is . . . ." She paused, adjusted her bracelets. "Well, let me check. Maybe I can find it." She went inside the house again.

Ben stole a quick glance at his mother. Her eyes were shut and he could see her hand clutching the Bible in her coat pocket.

"You want the bags?" the cab driver called to them. He had gotten out of the car to see what was delaying them.

"No, no . . ." Constance shook her head. "Just one more minute . . ."

They stood there dumbly, waiting for the woman to return. Even Felice didn't say a word.

At last the woman came to the door again and handed

11

Constance a piece of paper. "It's the address of the labor agency," she said. "Fortunately I'd kept the card in my desk. Check with them. Maybe they'll know where to find your husband." She stopped, looked embarrassed. "I wish I could help you more."

Constance folded the paper carefully and slipped it into her pocket. "Thank you very much, ma'am. I'm sorry to bother you." Constance's voice failed her again.

"You sure you're all right?" the woman said with concern. She looked beyond them to the taxi driver who was leaning up against his car, watching.

Constance nodded, took Jube's and then Felice's hand.

"You sure?" the woman said. "You're welcome to come in and use the phone. Or if you need money for cab fare . . ."

Ben felt his mother stiffen. "Thank you, but we're fine, ma'am," she said evenly. She turned and led her family quickly toward the cab.

The driver didn't seem particularly surprised to see the Gibsons return. He said nothing as he opened the door for Constance and then, once again, slid his huge body into the front seat.

Ben glanced back at the house as the cab turned around in the driveway. The woman was still standing in the doorway.

"So where to now?" the cabbie finally spoke as they started down the hill.

Constance shook her head and stared straight ahead at the cabbie's enormous shoulders. "I need to think on it," she said.

"How are we ever going to find Daddy now?" Felice asked, her eyes filling with tears.

The driver looked back at them in the rearview mirror. "Do you know anybody in L.A.?" he asked.

"Nobody," Constance said.

"And you don't have much money, right?"

Constance nodded.

"Then let me give you some advice, lady. Don't let the sunshine and the palm trees fool you. This is a hard city. Take the next bus back to wherever you came from."

Constance considered what he said. "We got things to do first. . . ." She took out the address the woman had given her and read it to him. "Is that back downtown?" she asked.

"A few blocks from the Greyhound station."

"I'm afraid I don't have the money for you to take us back there," she said.

"That's okay, lady. I'll take you to the nearest bus stop. The ride down the hill is free." Ben looked over at the meter and saw that the driver had never turned it on.

"Thanks. I 'preciate that," Constance said. She leaned back in the cab and shut her eyes.

2

"*I knew we shouldn't have come.*" *Felice scuffed the* sidewalk with her tennis shoe and glared at Constance.

"Did not," Ben retorted. "Didn't say a word about it." It was near noon and they were standing at a bus stop on Wilshire Boulevard where the taxi driver had dropped them off. Sleek, high-rise apartment buildings lined both sides of the streets.

"We should have known he wouldn't be here," Felice went on, kicking the sidewalk again for emphasis. "If he wanted us out here, he would have said so."

"Your daddy's not free with words like you," Constance said. "He don't always say what he's feeling."

"Well, how do you know he wants us back, then?" Felice demanded.

"Maybe he don't want *you* back," Ben said.

"Who says?" she snarled at him and thumped the pavement a few inches from his foot. Ben struck back and grazed her sneaker with his toe.

Constance stepped between them. "Stop it!" she

ordered. "I won't have you kicking at each other in the middle of the street."

"He started it," Felice argued, always quick to blame.

"Did not." Ben glared at her.

Jube tugged at his mother's sleeve. "I'm hungry," he whined. His rounded tummy reflected his constant appetite.

"You're always hungry," Ben snapped.

Constance rummaged in her shopping bag and found some crackers that she'd brought along from El Paso to keep Jube's stomach filled. She offered them to Ben and Felice as well.

Felice pushed them away. "I'm sick of crackers," she said sulkily.

"We didn't come all this way to be defeated by one little setback," Constance scolded her. "You got to have faith that things will work out all right."

Ben knew that she was right, that no matter what disappointments they'd suffered, in a moment everything could change. Even now his father might drive by in his Pontiac and see them standing at the bus stop. If they had enough faith, it was only a matter of time before they found each other again.

The bus arrived within a few minutes. Ben and Constance lugged their suitcases aboard. Ben dragged his bag up the aisle and fell into the first empty seat.

Constance and Jube sat a few seats back and Felice, still sulking, sat by herself near the rear, clutching her mop-haired doll to her chest. Ben stared out the window.

A sign announced that they were entering Beverly

Hills. The apartments gave way to bank buildings and stores displaying sequined evening gowns, furs, sports cars, oriental rugs. The shoppers on the palm-tree-lined street wore clothes as showy as the mannequins in the windows. It was hard for Ben to understand how some people could have so much and his family so little. Do rich folk have more faith than I do? he wondered.

God had made the earth for the poor as well as the rich, his mother had told him once. Sometimes he wasn't so sure. If there really was a God, Ben didn't understand why He'd turned His back on their family.

The bus passed through Beverly Hills and continued along the busy boulevard, past office buildings and department stores, churches and hotels, as if all the buildings one could imagine in a city had been laid out one after another along a single street. The passengers in the seats around Ben changed several times before his mother finally rose and signaled him that they had reached their stop. They had to transfer to one more bus to get to the employment agency.

The labor office was two blocks from the bus stop, in the older and dirtier part of downtown. The afternoon was warm and sunny and there were a number of men, and a few women, with faces leathery as lizards, hanging about the streets. Their ragged clothes and dull eyes made Ben think they didn't have much else to do but soak up the sun.

One man with a huge tear in the seat of his pants shadowboxed with a light post.

Two other men, and a woman in an oversized pea coat, leaned against a chain-link fence, drinking from a bottle in a crumpled paper bag. They stared at the Gibsons as they struggled past with their luggage. Ben kept his eyes on the pavement. Although his arm ached, he would not stop to rest. Not here.

One block later they had to step around a barefoot man curled up in the middle of the sidewalk. His feet and clothes were blackened with dirt and he smelled as sour as a cesspool. Constance looked at him with distaste and led Jube in a wide circle around the sleeping man.

"Phew!" Felice said in a loud whisper, holding her nose. Ben quickly looked around to see if any of the people on the street were watching them.

At last they reached The Right Man office, a small storefront protected by a folding metal gate. The gate was pulled back and the door open. Through the window Ben could see about a dozen men, of all colors, sitting in plastic chairs reading newspapers or napping. His father was not among them.

They entered the office and set their suitcases down by the front counter. An old cowboy movie was playing on a color television set mounted to the wall. The men in the chairs glanced at the Gibsons with little interest. An old man with a yellowed beard didn't even raise his head. He sat staring at his dirty toes through the holes of his tattered shoes.

"Can I help you?" A neatly dressed young man looked up at Constance from his desk. He wore a buttoned-down yellow shirt and a brown knit tie that further separated him from the grubby men on the other side of the counter.

Constance told him why she had come.

The man didn't recognize Clyde's name, but he

typed it into his computer to check. "Oh, you're right," he said after a moment. "We did hire him out. General cleanup. Four days this month."

"Do you have his address?" Constance said eagerly.

The man shook his head. "Afraid general delivery's all he listed."

"Where's that?" Constance asked.

"It's no place, really, just the post office. It's what the men put down when they're sleeping in their car . . . or in the streets."

Constance leaned heavily against the counter.

The man jumped up, perhaps afraid that she might topple over onto his desk. "Is this Clyde Gibson a relative of yours?" he asked.

"My husband."

He nodded as if he'd known it all along.

"Do you remember him?" Constance asked.

"Look, Mrs. Gibson, I get a hundred twenty to a hundred fifty men in here each week. Some of them are regulars who keep coming back, others just work a few days and move on. I see too many men a month to remember the ones who just pass through. Maybe if you had a picture . . ."

Constance opened her wallet and handed him the photograph.

As soon as he saw it, the man remembered Clyde. "Sure . . . big, strong fellow from Texas. Clean-shaven, polite. Easy to find work for. I was sorry when he didn't come back. . . ." He shrugged, as if it happened to him all the time.

Looking at the other men in the office, Ben could

understand why the labor contractor would remember his father. He was certain that, even at his most discouraged, Clyde Gibson never looked as sorry as these men.

"Do you know what happened to him?" Constance asked.

"Could be anything," the man said. "Everyone down here has their own reasons."

A handwritten sign on the wall hinted at what one of them might be: THIS IS NOT A BAR!!! KEEP IT OUTSIDE.

"Maybe somebody here knows him," the man suggested. "Clyde Gibson?" he asked loudly. "Anybody here know him?"

No one responded.

"Show them the picture," he encouraged Constance.

Constance hesitantly handed the snapshot to the nearest person, a young man with a soiled red headband. He stared at it with bloodshot eyes for at least a minute, then finally shook his head and passed it on. Ben could barely watch as the picture was passed from one dirty hand to another. He couldn't believe his father had been friendly with any of these men.

"A better time to come is around five in the morning," the man behind the counter explained when the photograph was returned, unrecognized. "That's when most of the men show up. If you come back then, you might have better luck."

Constance wrote down the general delivery address and thanked the man for his help.

"Can we leave now, Momma?" Felice asked. Ben realized it was the first time she'd spoken since they had entered the office. For once Ben was glad to hear her voice.

"If he comes by again, would you tell him his family was here looking for him?" Constance said.

"I sure will," the man said. "Where can he find you?"

"Well, we just got here," Constance said. "Can you recommend somewhere nearby to stay? We can't pay much. . . ."

The man shrugged. "I don't recommend any place around here, but you might try the Athens. Cross the street and head north. You can't miss it." He picked up the phone to answer a call. "The Right Man," he said brightly, turning his back to them as he sat down at his desk.

Ben felt a rush of relief to pick up the suitcase and leave the office. In a way he was glad his father hadn't returned. He didn't like to think of him sitting like those men, staring blankly at the TV, waiting for some rich lady to call for a hired hand to clean up the trash in her backyard.

3

ATHENS HOTEL

Newly Redecorated
$5 and up
Weekly–Monthly Rates
Clean–Quiet

Ben read the faded black letters painted in the white square on the brick wall of the three-story hotel. From the blurred condition of the sign, it looked to him as if the redecoration had been done a long time ago.

"What do you think?" Constance asked as they studied the building from across the street.

"It's pretty scuzzy," said Felice.

The place, indeed, appeared grim. The brick was sooty and weathered, and there were bars on the first floor windows, an iron gate guarding the front door, and barbed wire coils topping the chain-link fence of the parking lot. The building could have been a prison as easily as a hotel.

"Maybe it's better inside," Constance said. Ben guessed she was as tired and as hungry as he was. His arm ached from lugging the suitcase, and they hadn't eaten anything that day but crackers. The Athens didn't look any different from the other cheap hotels they'd passed.

Jube made the decision for them. "I got to pee," he said, squirming.

"Let's try this hotel, then," Constance said.

They crossed the street and walked to the entrance. The iron door was covered with heavy wire mesh. So was the front desk in the lobby.

Constance peered into a dark room behind the metal grating. A game show was playing on a small color television sitting on a shelf. Nobody appeared to be watching the screaming woman who had just won a trip to Hawaii. Constance rapped on the bars. "Anybody there?"

A completely shaven head rose from a chair just below the window. The man rubbed his eyes in apparent annoyance at being woken from his afternoon nap.

"Do you have any rooms?" Constance asked.

The man inspected the Gibsons through the wire window. He wore a feathered earring and had a serpent tattooed on his forearm. "For how long?" he asked.

"How much is it a night?"

"We only rent by the week."

"How much for the week, then?"

"The cheapest I've got is seventy-five bucks, in advance."

Constance hesitated.

"If you're looking for the Hilton, lady, it's six blocks uptown."

Jube yanked Constance's hand. "I got to go," he said. "Bad."

"Is there a bathroom my son can use?" Constance said.

"You see the sign?" The bald-headed man pointed to a cardboard sign on the wall behind her. Constance turned to read it: REST ROOMS ARE NOT FOR PUBLIC USE, SO PLEASE DON'T ASK.

"You going to take the room or not, lady?" the manager pressed.

Constance gave in. "I'll take it," she said. "Now where's the bathroom?"

"Through the door and down the end of the hall."

Constance nodded to Ben and he hurried off with Jube. When they found the bathroom, Ben had to hold his breath at the stench. The toilet looked and smelled as if it hadn't been cleaned in months.

By the time they returned, Constance had already paid for the week.

The manager helped them carry their bags to their third-floor room. Ben noticed the holes in the plaster as they climbed the stairs. Their room was at the far end of a dingy corridor, lit only by a single bulb. Sounds of radios or TV sets could be heard from behind a few of the closed doors. The only person they saw, though, was a young woman who eyed them from her open doorway as she tried to quiet a crying baby in her arms.

The manager dropped their bags in front of their room, inserted the key, and unlocked the door. "No cooking with hot plates," he warned. "And don't throw any trash in the halls or out the window," he added, as if

23

that was the first thing they were going to do. Then he turned and left them.

As they entered the room, a tiny animal shot across the floor and disappeared under one of the two beds.

"What was that?" Felice shrieked.

Jube immediately got down on his knees and stuck his head under the bed to find out. "A mouse!" he said with delight. "A little mouse!"

Felice clutched Millie to her chest and refused to budge another step. "I'm not sleeping in a room with a mouse."

"A mouse won't hurt you," Ben scoffed.

Felice shook her head adamantly. "Millie and I don't want him crawling over us when we sleep."

Constance put her arm around her daughter. "He's just as scared of you, honey, as you are of him."

"I don't care," said Felice.

"He's gone." Jube looked up in disappointment. "Ran away."

"See," Constance said.

The news didn't make Felice any happier. She buried her face against Constance's breast. "Millie thinks this is a terrible place," she said.

Looking around the tiny room, barely wide enough to hold both beds, Ben felt the same way. The mattresses of the unmade beds were both stained and discolored, the porcelain sink chipped and rusty. The dresser tilted on a broken leg. Ben went over to the window and raised the torn shade. A part of the glass had been broken and sloppily mended with cardboard and tape. The window looked out on a fire escape and an alley littered with garbage.

Ben turned back to the room. In the light from the window he could see that the spots on the sickly green walls were dead roaches, squashed by former residents and left there, like graffiti. He watched his mother take in the roaches on the crumbling walls, the broken window, the cracked and buckling linoleum floor. As she sat down on the edge of the sagging bed, the bedsprings creaked. "It's only for a week," she said finally.

Ben swallowed hard to keep down the disgust rising in his throat. As far as they had fallen in El Paso, they'd never had to live like this. But he could put up with it for a few days to find his father.

His mother, too, had not come all this way to let a few bugs and dirt defeat her. "What this place needs is a good scrubbing," she declared.

Opening her wallet, she carefully counted out eight one-dollar bills from their dwindling supply of money and handed them to Ben with instructions to pick up some sponges and ammonia from the nearest market. "That shouldn't cost much more than a dollar," she explained. "Use the rest for food. Get a loaf of bread, some peanut butter, jelly . . . a small pack of cheese slices if they have them, some Kool Aid. . . . Oh, and some paper cups . . ."

"Cookies," Jube added. "I want cookies."

"No cookies," Constance said sharply. "We don't have money to waste on sweets. We have to count our pennies till we find your daddy."

She made Ben repeat the shopping list to be sure he got it right. "Now you be careful," she added. "Straight to the store and straight back."

"I want to go with him," Felice said eagerly.

"No, you stay with me," Constance said.

"Why?" Felice asked, ignoring the edginess in her mother's voice.

" 'Cause I want you here," Constance said in a tone that cut off any argument.

Ben understood his mother's nervousness. The streets around the hotel had frightened him, too, but his mother depended on his help and he wasn't about to let her down. After all, the idea to come to L.A. had been his as much as hers.

He stuffed the bills deep into the front pocket of his jeans and, assuring Constance once more that he'd be careful, set out for the store.

The hotel manager directed him to the nearest market, which was only two blocks away. Following his instructions, Ben turned the corner by the hotel. The street seemed to be a kind of neighborhood gathering place. Both sides were lined with men and women lounging against the graffiti-covered buildings. Ben didn't see any children. Shoving the money deeper into his pocket, he started tensely down the street. The stink was almost as strong as the toilet at the hotel.

Some of the idlers stood chatting and drinking from paper bags, others sat on wooden crates or overturned shopping carts. A few reclined on tattered couches, whose stuffing spilled out the sides like garbage from a split trash bag.

"Hey, sport, want to pitch for pennies?" a shirtless man with a jagged scar on his chest called to Ben as he approached. "C'mon, try your luck," he invited, pointing to a crude circle chalked on the sidewalk. To demonstrate he flipped a penny, which landed smack in the center of the circle. The man flashed a chip-toothed grin.

Ben quickened his pace.

"Hey, amigo, got some money?" another voice called from a doorway. "Want to feel good? Try some dust? Some weed?"

Ben kept his eyes on the street ahead of him and hurried on.

He passed a man muttering to himself and shooing away invisible flies. Another sat in the middle of the pavement staring blankly at the broken glass on the sidewalk. A pretty young woman in red shorts and matching high heels danced by herself to the music of a portable radio while an old man in a torn overcoat ranted at her about "the preachers and politicians who murdered Jesus."

Ben thought of the fiery sermons his mother's minister gave about hell and wondered if he had ever walked this street in Los Angeles.

At last Ben arrived at Bill's Market. Its front shelves were all stocked with liquor. The food and groceries took up the back of the store.

Ben quickly found the items on his mother's list. Eight dollars didn't go very far in this store. Adding up the cost of the cleaning supplies, the paper cups, and food, he had less than a dollar left to buy some overripe bananas. He waited in line while a man in dirt-stiffened clothes bought two loose cigarettes for twenty-five cents each. Then the clerk totaled Ben's purchases on the cash register and handed him a quarter change.

On the way back to the hotel, Ben tried a different

route. There were fewer people loitering on this street, but the smell of alcohol was stronger, drifting from the open doorways of the bars and mingling with the odor of rotting garbage in the gutters. An old man, with a face paler than his tangled white hair, staggered out the doorway of a tavern and lurched toward Ben as he approached. Ben darted across the street to avoid him. Looking back, he saw the man leaning against a parking meter, vomiting into the street.

A siren wailed and a police car sped past. No doubt on the way to more important problems than a sick old wino, Ben thought. He watched the drunk right himself, wipe his mouth with the sleeve of his jacket, and zigzag back toward the entrance to the bar.

A heaviness settled in Ben's chest like a barbell. Surely his father hadn't come to the city of dreams to live like this. If he was still in L.A., Ben was confident that his father was miles away from this part of the city.

As he turned toward the Athens again, Ben saw a thin black man with a grizzled beard staring at him from behind a trash can. "What's the matter, boy?" the man asked. "Ain't you ever seen a genuine in-e-bri-ate before?"

Ben was too startled to reply. The man must have been watching him for a while. He wore a red ski cap, a discolored T-shirt, and red suspenders that held up a pair of baggy black pants several sizes too large.

"Ain't no one ever told you? It ain't polite to gape," the tramp went on as he calmly rooted through the garbage.

Ben watched with horror as the trash picker pulled a half-eaten sandwich from the can and held it up to

28

examine. As poor as the Gibsons were, they'd never dug through the garbage for food.

Ben reached into his pocket and pulled out the change from the market. "Here," he offered.

The man looked at him in surprise. "You want to buy this sandwich?"

"No, it's for you." Ben held out the quarter.

The tramp scowled. "I don't take no money from kids."

"No, keep it," Ben said, flinging the coin at him in embarrassment. The quarter bounced off the red suspenders and into the trash.

The scavenger just stared at him.

Ben tucked his grocery sack under his arm and ran. He didn't even look back to see if the man had recovered the quarter. If he could eat other people's garbage, what would keep him from plunging his hands to the bottom of the barrel to find some money?

4

When Ben returned with the groceries, Constance passed out the slices of cheese but put away the rest of the food until they had cleaned the room. Ben and Felice took turns helping their mother scour the walls clean of roaches. Constance scrubbed so hard that she scraped away whole patches of green paint. Then, red-faced and perspiring, she attacked the window and the sink and the closet and finally the rickety dresser, making Ben carry each of the drawers to the window to dump the bugs outside. Only when the sponges began to fall apart and the bottle of ammonia was empty was she willing to stop. The air burned with disinfectant and the bruised walls looked even more scarred than before, but his mother was finally satisfied that the room was clean enough to eat and sleep in.

Using her pink flannel bathrobe for a tablecloth, she covered the suitcase and set out a dinner of peanut butter and jelly sandwiches and the bananas that Ben had brought from the market. Although Ben didn't see much to be thankful for, his mother made them bow

30

their heads and say grace before they ate their meager meal.

"Is this all?" Jube asked, his mouth thick with peanut butter.

"You can have as many sandwiches as you want," Constance said.

Despite his earlier hunger, Ben found himself with little appetite now. He kept thinking of the man he'd seen raiding the trash can. He noticed his mother barely touched her food, either.

After dinner they shook the crumbs from Constance's bathrobe out the window, wrapped the food to protect it from the roaches, and slid the suitcase-table under the bed. It was still not dark yet when they had finished cleaning up. There were hours to go before bedtime and little to occupy themselves with in the hotel room.

Constance took out her Bible, Jube his plastic firetruck, and Felice her doll. Ben put on his jacket and went out to the fire escape outside their room. The night air was a little cool, but on the landing he could at least escape the ammonia fumes. He took out the harmonica his father had given him for his eleventh birthday and began to play. Although he knew a fair number of songs, often he enjoyed making up his own tunes more, playing around with whatever notes or melodies popped into his head. Sometimes what came out surprised him; he discovered things in the music he didn't even know were inside him, feelings he often couldn't put into words. It was easy to lose himself in his playing. Hours would pass almost without notice.

Now, sitting on the iron fire escape, dangling his feet over the garbage-strewn alley below, Ben shut his eyes and tried to imagine himself somewhere else, like the Mountain Fork River where he and his father had gone fishing in Oklahoma the previous summer. Fiddling with the harmonica Ben tried to find a tune that would recapture the feeling of that trip. But tonight all the notes he blew came out shrill and jangly.

"Can't you play something nice?" Felice came to the window to complain. "You sound worse than Jube crying."

Ben brayed at her with the harmonica. "Then shut your ears," he said. But he turned to more familiar tunes, "The Yellow Rose of Texas" and "Streets of Laredo." He didn't like other people listening to him when he improvised. It made him feel self-conscious, as if they were eavesdropping on his private thoughts.

As night fell, Ben watched the lights go on in the other hotel rooms. From time to time someone would appear at a window to see where the music was coming from. They would nod or smile at him or turn away without interest. A boy of about six or seven stood at his window a long time listening. No matter what song Ben chose, the boy's grave expression never changed. Ben wondered what had happened to make him so cheerless. Had his family fallen on hard times, too?

At last Constance called him inside to help get Jube ready for bed and take him to the bathroom. The one toilet on the floor was occupied and Ben waited with Jube in the hallway until it was free. Just as the bathroom door opened, a gangly youth, wearing a New York Yankee cap turned backward, stepped into the hall.

"I'm next, dude," he said, pushing in front of them.

Before Ben could argue, the boy entered the bathroom and slammed the door.

"We were first," Jube protested, quivering.

"I know," Ben said quietly.

"You tell him," Jube urged.

"I don't think he cares," Ben answered. He decided not to retreat to the second-floor bathroom. He was too curious about the boy with the baseball cap, the only person his own age he'd seen around the Athens.

When the boy came out of the bathroom, he stopped to size Ben up. "You never know what lowlife's gonna turn up in this dump," he said.

"You're the one who cut in." Ben's voice almost stuck in his throat.

"You want to make something of it?" The youth was a head taller than Ben and looked a lot tougher.

"I just want to take my little brother to the bathroom," Ben said, pushing past him.

"What's the matter? He gonna fall in without you?" The boy laughed.

"Why's he so mean?" Jube asked when the two of them were safely locked inside.

"I don't know," Ben said, "but he surely is."

When they emerged from the toilet, a young black woman was waiting in the hall in a yellow robe and curlers.

"You new here?" she asked with interest.

"Yes, ma'am," Ben mumbled.

"Where you from, child?"

"El Paso."

"We're here looking for our daddy," Jube volunteered.

"Ain't we all, honey," she said. "Ain't we all." She patted Jube on the head and entered the bathroom.

Within ten minutes after they'd returned to their

room, Jube had curled up on a bed and fallen asleep. A half hour later, exhausted from the day's ordeal, they were all ready to join him.

Constance turned out the bedroom light and got into bed with Felice and Millie. Ben crawled under the scratchy sheets and gently pushed his sleeping brother to the edge of the mattress. Their single bed was barely big enough for both of them and Ben lay there stiffly, listening to the sounds of the hotel—the dripping of the faucet in the sink, the slamming of doors, the footsteps of people passing back and forth in the corridor. The walls were so thin he could even hear the mice (or were they rats?) skittering and squeaking behind them.

"Are you sure a mouse won't crawl over me when I sleep?" Felice asked. Ben guessed she was afraid to close her eyes.

"If you're worrying about it, sleep way down under the covers," Constance suggested.

Felice tried it for a minute. "It's too smothery," she said, coming up for air.

"Then sleep sitting up," Constance whispered. "No mouse is going to climb up you."

Watching Felice rearrange her pillow in the dark, Ben thought he might be more comfortable sleeping upright as well, so he folded his pillow into a backrest, too. "What about the bugs?" Felice asked when she had finally settled down in her new position.

"They don't eat people," Constance assured her.

Ben heard his sister fiddle with the covers all over again. Apparently, she was not so sure.

In the next room a man and woman began to argue in Spanish. Touching the wall beside him, Ben could feel it vibrating with their shouting. He was glad he couldn't understand what they were saying. When his parents used to fight, he would bury his head under his pillow so that he couldn't hear.

"Tell us a story, Momma," Felice begged.

"What kind of story?" Constance asked.

"Something funny," Felice said.

"When you were living on the ranch," Ben added. Constance's mother had died when Constance was seven, and she had lived with her father on a west Texas cattle ranch where he was foreman. The years she grew up there often seemed to Ben the happiest of her life. When she turned thirteen, though, her father sent her back to town to live with an aunt because he didn't think a cattle ranch was a proper place to raise a young girl.

Constance was silent a moment. "I was remembering today how Mr. Withers got saved."

"The man who owned the ranch?" Felice asked.

"May he rest in peace," Constance said.

"Tell us about him, Momma," Ben urged. Although he had heard the story several times before, it was one of his favorites.

"Well, I guess I've told you that Mr. Withers liked to drink," she started, sitting up in bed. "But Mrs. Withers, well, she didn't approve and wouldn't let him bring even a can of beer into the house. So Mr. Withers would hide his liquor out on the range. At night, when he felt a hankering for a drink, he'd go out 'to check for rustlers' or 'to look in on a sick calf.' Now Mrs. Withers was as smart as her husband and knew exactly what he was up to. But one year his drinking got so bad, she decided to put a stop to it.

"It was a terrible drought that year. Six months with-

35

out a drop of rain. The drier it grew, the thirstier Mr. Withers got. So one Saturday Mrs. Withers invited me up to the house for lunch and offered me a job. I was about a year younger than Ben, and it was the first paying job I'd ever had. For every bottle her husband hid that I tracked down, she'd give me a dime.

"Well, I tell you, it wasn't long before I had a shoe box full of dimes. The ranch was four sections, and, believe me, every few acres, behind a rock or cactus, Mr. Withers had planted a bottle. Every afternoon I'd come home from school, saddle up my horse, and ride out looking for them. It was like going on a treasure hunt every day. The more bottles I found, the smarter he got at hiding them. But I knew from Mrs. Withers that I was winning the game 'cause when her husband went out at night 'to check for rustlers,' he'd come back as mean and ornery as if he'd actually met one.

"Now one day the minister came out to the ranch and Mr. Withers and my daddy drove him 'round in the pickup to show him just how bad things were. Every five minutes Mr. Withers would stop the truck and get out to check behind a bush or cactus for 'signs of rustlers.' But I'd been doing my job pretty well and he couldn't find a single bottle. The farther he drove, the angrier he got. 'What I'd do for a drop of wetness,' he said to my father. Well, the preacher thought that he meant rain, and he said why don't we stop the truck right here and now and kneel down and pray for it. Mr. Withers figured he had nothing to lose, so he said why not. But when they'd all knelt down, the preacher said that God might look more favorably on their prayers if they promised Him something in return. Mr. Withers looked up in the blazing sky and didn't see a single cloud. So he said, 'Well, if it rains today, I'll give up drinking for good.' The preacher said that was a big sacrifice indeed and would certainly make God listen to their prayers.

"When they finished praying they all rose, and what did Mr. Withers see but a flask that he had hidden months before and forgotten all about. My daddy saw it, too, but he didn't let on anything. They all got into the truck and Mr. Withers said, 'Wait a minute, I think I dropped my pocket knife back there. You stay here, I'll go look for it.' He got out to pick up his whiskey, but just as he went for it, he heard a hissing. A rattler was coiled around the bottle ready to strike. Mr. Withers didn't think twice. He just pulled his gun and fired. At the same time that he blasted the snake, he blew the whiskey bottle apart. When he saw what he'd done, he sat down on the ground and cried like a baby.

"The preacher said it was a sign from the Lord, a warning of the poison of alcohol. It surely put the fear of God into Mr. Withers. After that, he never touched another drop of drink."

"It rained that night, didn't it?" said Felice, who had heard the story before, too.

"Not that night," Constance said, "the next morning. We awoke at dawn to the sound of thunder, and we all went outside and soaked ourselves in the rain."

They were all silent for a moment. Ben thought of how much his father had begun to drink after he'd lost his job. He wondered if his mother was thinking the same thing.

The voices rose again in the next room. The woman's was shrill and frightened.

"Do you think we need to promise God something

for Him to bring Daddy back to us?" Felice asked.

"I think all God asks of us is that we do the best we can," Constance said, "and we keep our faith in Him. As long as we do that, I'm sure that one day the Lord will answer our prayers."

Like a clap of thunder, a slap sounded sharply through the walls. A few seconds later the woman in the next room began crying. They listened to her in silence.

"I hope the Lord hears us soon," Felice said at last.

"I keep praying that He will," Constance said. "Remember what it says in Psalms: 'Weeping may endure for a night, but joy cometh in the morning.' "

Like his father, Ben didn't have much faith in prayer or churchgoing, but as he closed his eyes, he prayed that when he woke tomorrow the Lord would bring joy to both the woman sobbing next door and his family.

5

With a start Ben sprang up in bed. For an instant, in the dark, he couldn't remember where he was. Then his eyes adjusted to the faint illumination from the street lamp filtering through the torn window shade and he discovered his mother in the far corner of the room, pulling a sweater over her head. Perhaps the rustle of her clothes as she dressed had awakened him.

Seeing him sit up, she came over to the bed and touched his cheek. "Bad dream?" she asked softly.

He shook his head. His dreams had been of fishing with his father on the Mountain Fork River. What had frightened him was waking to find himself in the hotel. "Why are you dressed?" he whispered.

"I told you last night. I'm going back to the labor agency."

"But it's still dark," he said.

"The man said the best time was at five, when they opened."

"Let me come with you," he said, swinging his feet to the cold linoleum floor.

"No." She put her hand on his shoulder to stop him.

"I can't leave Felice and Jube alone. I need you to look after them."

"We can take them with us," he said.

"No, it's better if they sleep," she said firmly. "You, too."

He didn't like staying alone at the hotel, but he knew there was no choice. Ever since his father's disappearance, Constance had depended on him to take charge when she was gone.

"I'll try not to be long," she said.

Jube flopped over onto his stomach beside Ben. Constance waited a minute to be sure he stayed asleep, then quietly took out her wallet and removed several bills. "I don't want to carry all this money with me on the street," she said. Sliding the suitcase from under Ben's bed, she pulled out a sock, stuffed the money inside, and buried it at the bottom of the bag. "That should keep it safe," she said, shoving the suitcase back under the bed. She kissed Ben on the forehead. "Now go to sleep. I'll only be a little while."

Ben watched as, carrying her loafers in her hand to keep from rousing Jube and Felice, she carefully opened the door and slipped into the hallway. He could hear her outside the doorway putting on her shoes and then walking quickly down the hall.

After she left, Ben found it difficult to get back to sleep. Since his father had lost his job, Ben often found himself waking in the middle of the night, his stomach knotted with worry about what was going to happen to his family. To keep from thinking of their growing poverty—the kitchen drawer stuffed with bills that his father didn't even bother opening anymore—he would try to remember the good times they used to have together. Family barbecues in the park by the Rio Grande. Singing together as they drove across the border on shopping trips to Juárez. Sitting on his father's workbench in the garage, watching him work on his '69 Pontiac. And of course the Oklahoma fishing trip the two of them had made together.

Whenever he couldn't sleep he'd try to revive one of these favorite memories, to imagine them as vividly as he could, as if the more details he could remember, the more chance he could make them happen again. This morning he tried to conjure up the fishing trip. After months of idleness, his father had finally been promised a job in a garage and, to celebrate, had taken Ben fishing with him. Ben could recall almost everything about the trip: from the hot breeze as they drove shirtless across the Texas grasslands, their bare backs sticking to the vinyl seats, to the chill, rushing waters of the Mountain Fork as he and his father waded hip-deep into the river. He remembered his father's damp hair on his cheek as he reached his burly arms around him to help steady his rod and pull in the biggest bass either of them had ever caught. . . .

This morning, though, Ben couldn't hold any of these images in his mind. The cramped bed and its gritty sheets kept pulling him back to the shabby hotel room, reminding him of the bitterness of their return to El Paso when his father learned that the job he'd been promised had been given to someone with more experience.

After a while Ben gave up his attempts to sleep and went over to the window. Dawn had broken, as gray as dishwater, over the bottle-strewn alley. Staring out the window, Ben watched an old man, draped in a ragged blanket, hobble down the alley. He stopped by the overflowing hotel dumpster, suddenly undid his trousers, and squatted to relieve himself. Ben quickly turned away.

Felice was stretching sleepily in her bed. "What are you looking at?" she asked.

"*Nothing*," he said sharply.

She propped herself on her elbows to get a better view.

"Yecch!" she said with repulsion.

Her outburst woke Jube. He looked around the room in confusion. "Where's Momma?" he asked.

"She went out," Ben told him.

Jube started to cry. "I don't like it here."

"Nobody does," said Felice.

Ben went over to his brother and tried to comfort him. "Don't cry," he said, rocking Jube back and forth. "Momma will be back soon."

"I want her now," he sobbed.

"Give him some peanut butter and jelly," Felice, practical as usual, suggested. "That'll shut him up."

"How about a sandwich?" Ben asked, getting up to make him one.

But this morning, not even food could console him. "I want Momma," he wailed.

A fist banged against the other side of the wall, from the same room where they had heard the woman crying. "Shut that damn kid up!" a male voice shouted.

The pounding stunned them all into silence. Ben held his breath.

Frightened now, Jube cried even louder.

"If you don't shut that brat up, I sure as hell will," the man warned.

"Please," Ben begged his brother. "Please stop."

But Jube had lost any control. His plump body heaved and shuddered.

Ben glanced helplessly at the door, waiting for the man in the next room to burst through it.

"Do something!" Felice pleaded, her face pale with terror.

Desperate, Ben grabbed a pillow from the bed and shoved it in Jube's face. "Bite on it!" he ordered. "Hard!"

Jube tried to do what Ben commanded. The effort momentarily distracted him and the pillow helped muffle his sobbing.

Ben sat down next to him on the bed and gently rubbed Jube's back. "Take a deep breath," he guided. "That's it. Breathe deeply and bite the pillow."

Felice sat on Jube's other side and held his hand. "It's going to be okay, Jubie. It's going to be okay," she kept repeating.

All three stared at the door, waiting.

Gradually Jube stopped crying, though his trembling took as long to subside as the pounding of Ben's heart.

They did not hear again from the man next door.

Constance returned a few hours later with doughnuts and good news. She had met a man at the labor agency who knew their father. His name was Randall and he had worked a day with Clyde Gibson clearing brush. Clyde had told him he was staying in one of the hotels near the bus station, although Randall wasn't sure which one. He knew his way around that part of the city, though, and had agreed to meet Constance later that afternoon and take her to the places where Clyde might be living.

Jube was more interested in the doughnuts than the news, but Felice and Ben were both excited by Constance's discovery. "He really knows Daddy?" Felice said.

"That's what he said, honey." Constance smiled.

"Can we go with you to find him?" Felice asked.

Constance shook her head. "I don't know how far it is," she said. "It's better if you stay here. I promise you, as soon as I find your daddy, I'll bring him back here."

Ben didn't say anything to her about Jube's hysterics or the man in the next room. If she found Clyde that afternoon, they'd be leaving the hotel, anyway. "Did the man say how Daddy is?" Ben asked.

"He didn't know him real well," Constance answered. "He only worked with him a day." She took off her shoes and lay back on the bed. "Maybe the Lord is finally ready to answer our prayers."

Please, God, may it be this afternoon, Ben offered a short, silent prayer of his own.

Constance yawned and hugged Jube, who snuggled next to her on the bed. "I'm worn down," she said. "I'm going to try to catch a little sleep."

Ben couldn't stand the thought of spending the rest of the day in the hotel room, waiting. "Can I go outside?" he asked.

"Me, too," Felice jumped in.

Reluctantly Constance let them go. "Only if you stay

close by," she cautioned. "I don't want you wandering off anywhere." They quickly got their jackets before she could change her mind. Jube was happy to stay behind and have his mother to himself.

Outside the hotel, though, there was little more to do than in their room. They had neither ball nor jump rope, and they saw no other children playing on the street. Either they're all at school, Ben thought, or else few children live downtown.

"Why don't we explore a little?" Ben ventured.

"You heard what Momma said," Felice reminded him.

"We'll just go a few blocks. That isn't far."

Felice hesitated.

"Maybe we'll see Daddy," he enticed her.

"Okay," she gave in, "but if we get into trouble I'm telling Momma that you made me."

"We won't get into trouble," he promised.

They set off in the opposite direction from the market. Ben had no desire to walk that street again.

A block from the hotel they stopped to peer in the doorway of a wholesale toy store. Ben looked over Felice's shoulder at the stacks of boxes of cheap imported toys. "Even the dolls look sad here," she said, turning away. "Millie wouldn't want to play with any of them."

Continuing down the street, they passed a Latino man and woman and two small children carrying flimsy cardboard suitcases tied together with rope. In El Paso Ben had seen other families like them who had crossed the border hoping to find a better life in the United States. He wondered if this family had come to L.A. for the same reason and if they were as disappointed as his own by what they'd found.

"Let's go back," Felice said when they had reached the corner. "There's nothing here."

Ben had to agree. The boarded-up buildings and the vacant, fenced-in lots showed that others had long since given up on that part of the city.

He led Felice across the street and they turned back toward the hotel. As they neared the alley, an unshaven man with a jagged scar across his forehead stepped out of the doorway of a deserted pawnshop. "You spare some change, kid?" He blocked the sidewalk in front of them.

A half step behind Ben, Felice clutched his belt. There were two other men huddling in the dark doorway.

Ben stuck his hands in his empty pockets. If he'd had any coins he would gladly have handed them over to get past.

"I—I don't have any money," he stammered.

The man didn't budge. "What else you got?" he demanded.

The only thing of value Ben carried was the harmonica in his jacket pocket. "Nothing," he choked.

The man didn't believe him. "Let me see those pockets," he said, stepping close enough so that Ben could smell the liquor on his breath.

Ben glanced up the street for help, but he saw no one near except the men in the doorway. He turned out the two front pockets of his jeans, producing only some crumpled tissues. "See," he said.

"What about your jacket?" Ben felt Felice's grip tighten on his belt. He readied himself to run.

"Let him alone," a voice called from the doorway. "He got nothing but lint in those pockets." A man emerged from the shadows. Ben recognized his red ski cap and red suspenders from the day before.

"You know these kids, Nick?" the other man said in surprise.

"Yeah, I met the boy before."

The scar-faced man spit into the alley in disgust. "Well I never seen him around."

"They new down here I expect. That right, boy?"

"Yessir," Ben mumbled.

"Yessir." Scarface mimicked his reply. "He sure don't talk like he's from around here."

"Where you from, boy?" Nick asked.

"Texas."

"That your sister, Tex?"

Ben nodded.

"How long you living down here on skid row?"

"Two days," Ben answered.

"Didn't nobody tell you yet that this ain't a good neighborhood for kids?"

"Nosir." Ben stared at a hole in the leg of Nick's baggy pants.

"Well, I'm going to explain something to you kids." Nick motioned them closer. Ben moved a step nearer but still left some distance between them. Felice kept her grip on Ben's belt.

"You don't trust me, do you?" Nick said to her.

"We don't know you," Felice replied.

"That's right, you don't, girl. And even if you did, I still wouldn't trust me. That's Nick's first rule for survival on the streets. Don't trust nobody. Right?" He turned to his buddies to back him up.

"You tell 'em, bro," the other man in the doorway replied.

"You kids going to live down here, you going to have to toughen up," Nick went on. "You want to make it on the row, you better follow Nick's golden rules for survival. Don't trust nobody. And always keep your running shoes on. 'Cause you never know when someone's going to turn on you." He suddenly struck the air with a karate chop and gave them a cruel, squint-eyed stare. Both Ben and Felice backed away.

"You see what I'm saying?" Nick grinned, exposing two missing teeth in his lower jaw. "Maybe I just be acting now, but tomorrow I could mean it."

Scarface spat again. "What you wasting your breath on these kids for? They want to play around here, let them take their chances."

"The boy done me a favor yesterday," Nick replied. "I just be paying him back."

"Well now you're even," Scarface said. With a sudden roar he unleashed a fierce karate chop in Ben's direction.

This time Ben didn't wait to make up his mind. Grabbing Felice's hand, he ran. The men's laughter followed them all the way down the block.

6

Constance didn't find her husband that Tuesday after-
noon. Although she and Randall asked at all the hotels
within four blocks of the Greyhound station, none of
the desk clerks remembered Clyde or found his name
listed in their registries. "Randall felt awful bad," Constance reported to her children when she returned to
the Athens. "He was sure your daddy was staying near
the bus station, but maybe he misremembered what
Daddy said."

Despite their failure, Randall had offered to go with
Constance the next day to the missions, the church-run
shelters where a single man could get a bed for the
night and three hot meals if he lined up early enough in
the morning.

The way his father felt about churches, Ben didn't
think he'd be staying at a mission. His dad would spend
the night in his car before he'd suffer through a sermon
to get a bed.

"Why are you looking in the missions?" Ben asked.

"Most of those hotels we saw, they're even worse

than this one. A mission's at least free. Randall says lots of men use them for a few nights."

He didn't know about this Randall. "How come he's willing to help you look for Daddy?" Ben asked.

"He's a good Christian man who knows what it's like to be down on your luck," Constance answered.

Ben still didn't understand why Randall was so ready to go out of his way for Constance, or why his usually proud mother was so willing to let him help.

He thought of Nick's first rule of survival—don't trust anybody—but he could sense that it would anger his mother to repeat it to her. Besides, maybe she was right and Randall was just acting out of Christian kindness. He had, in fact, lent her a can opener and other kitchen utensils as well as given her a few canned goods and groceries. For dinner that night they ate applesauce and cold beets with their peanut butter sandwiches.

On Wednesday morning Constance rose early to continue her search with Randall.

"Take us with you," Felice begged.

Constance wouldn't even consider it. "These are no places to be dragging children. It's safer for you here in the hotel."

"But there's nothing to do here," Felice complained.

"I'll bring you back some cards," Constance promised.

Felice folded her doll's arms across her chest and tilted Millie's freckled face to display her defiance. "Millie doesn't play cards," she said.

Constance patted Millie's upturned head. "What would Millie like?" she asked.

"To go back to El Paso," Felice quickly answered.

Constance moved her hand from the doll's head to Felice's. "I know it's hard," she said. "I know."

She put on her worn brown coat, kissed them all good-bye, and left the room. Ben felt as resentful as his sister listening to his mother's footsteps disappear down the hall. He knew he could do more to help find his father than baby-sitting.

"I want to go outside and play," Jube said when Constance had gone.

"We can't," Ben said. His mother had given him strict instructions to remain in the room, which he'd promised to obey. She counted on him, and he wasn't going to disappoint her.

"Why?" Jube asked. "Why can't we go outside?"

"Because there are mean old men out there who eat little children," Felice warned darkly.

Jube's bottom lip began to quiver. He looked at Ben. "That's not true, is it, Ben?"

"No, she's just teasing." Ben gave Felice an angry look. "But Momma wants us to stay inside till she gets back."

To pass the time they made up games, pitching pennies at a paper cup, spitting water from the fire escape, and trapping roaches—"uckies," Felice called them. Although she refused to catch any herself, she cheered every one that Jube gleefully squashed.

Constance returned to the hotel room around noon with oranges, cheese spread, a fresh loaf of bread, and an old deck of cards (another present from Randall). Once again she'd had no luck finding Clyde. At the post office, though, she'd met another man picking up mail at general delivery who recognized Clyde's picture and said he'd worked with him doing yardwork a few weeks before. But the man had no idea where to find him now.

"At least people around here have seen him," she said with more encouragement than she'd shown the day before. Still, she didn't go out anymore that day.

In the afternoon she made Ben and Felice take Jube outside for some fresh air. After Felice's earlier warning, though, it took some coaxing to get Jube to leave the hotel.

"Where are the swings?" he asked as he surveyed the bleak, dirty street. In El Paso they had often gone to a park near their house.

"They don't have swings around here," Ben said.

"Not in the whole city?" Jube said in amazement.

"Not where we are."

"How about a jungle gym?"

"This isn't a playground," Felice said, kicking an empty wine bottle into the street. "It's a garbage dump."

They looked around the trash-filled street. The only people in sight this afternoon were a few men unloading a furniture truck in the warehouse parking lot across from the hotel.

"How about kick the can?" Ben suggested, spotting an empty beer can on the sidewalk. Nobody had a better idea, so they kicked the can back and forth awhile until Ben finally sent it sailing into the street, where it landed in a mess of broken bottles and wet paper that someone must have hosed from the sidewalk earlier. Ben, Felice, and Jube stood at the curb, gazing at the huge, black water bugs crawling over the soggy garbage: old clothes, rotten fruit, discarded paper plates with sodden clumps of beans left on them. No one made a move to retrieve the can. "It's too dirty to play here," Jube said, reaching for Ben's hand. "Let's go back."

When they returned to the room, even Felice was happy to play cards.

Later that evening, after they had eaten another dinner of cold sandwiches, Felice came out to the fire escape where Ben was playing his harmonica. She sat next to him on the metal landing and sang the words of the songs she knew or hummed softly to the ones she didn't. They sat there a long time in the dark.

"Do you think Daddy's living down here?" she asked at last.

"Not in a rat hole like this," he said. He looked over his shoulder to see if Constance had heard, but she wasn't near the window.

"I don't think Momma's going to find him around here, either," Felice whispered. He was glad to know that she agreed with him.

"Where do you think he is?" she said after a while.

"I don't know. Maybe he got work and stayed around that woman's house in the hills," he said hopefully.

"Maybe." She didn't sound convinced.

"Or maybe he's living near the ocean—wherever that is."

"That's where I'd go," she said.

"Yeah, he might be on the beach right now, fishing." Clyde's rod and tackle and some tools were about the only things he'd taken with him when he left.

"Do you think we could get Momma to look out there?" she said.

"Not as long as she listens to this guy Randall." Ben couldn't understand why she trusted a stranger to find Clyde more than she did her own children.

"Well, we could look for him ourselves. What do you think?" Felice said excitedly.

"The beach is way too far from here."

"Well, what about uptown, in the nice part?" she said. "If Daddy's staying in a hotel, maybe he's at one of those big ones we saw coming in on the bus."

"They have to be pretty expensive," Ben said.

"Well, maybe he has a job," Felice persisted. "A real good one . . ."

"Maybe," he conceded. He'd always believed that one day his father's luck was going to change.

"Sure," she said. "That's why he didn't come back to that Right Man place."

"Yeah . . ." The more he thought about it, the more possible it seemed. His father couldn't have sent them a hundred dollars unless he had a job. And if he were working steadily, he certainly could afford to live somewhere better than around the bus station. "I guess he could be at one of those hotels," Ben said, beginning to see that it might be true.

"We should look for him there," Felice said softly.

"By ourselves?"

"Tomorrow, when Momma goes out," she whispered.

"I don't know," he said. It was one thing to wander a few blocks from the hotel, another to wander around uptown when they were supposed to stay in their room. "There are a lot of hotels to check, and we'd have to take Jube with us."

"He won't care."

"What if he tells Momma?"

"If we find Daddy, she'll forgive us."

"I'll think about it," Ben said. Before he made up his mind he wanted to talk to his mother.

He waited until Jube and Felice had fallen asleep and his mother had finished studying her Bible. She put the book away carefully in her purse, turned off the overhead light, and came over to Ben's bed. "Hard to sleep?" she asked, running her warm hand over his forehead.

"I've been thinking about Daddy," he said.

"I know you have." Constance sat down on the edge of the bed.

"Do you think we're going to find him?"

"I keep praying that we will." She smoothed the covers around him.

"If you pray for Daddy's luck to change, how come you keep looking for him in flophouses and shelters?" he asked.

Constance withdrew her hand from his blanket. "That's where people live down here."

"But what if he's someplace else?"

"The man I met today and Randall both saw him around here."

"I think he's left," Ben said, sitting up in bed. "I think he's found some work and moved."

Constance stared at the pale glow from the street lamp in the alley. "I hope you're right," she said. "I certainly do, but the only way I know to find your daddy now is to look down here, because that's the last place anybody saw him." She brushed the hair back from his forehead. "Now you try to get some sleep. Maybe tomorrow we'll meet somebody who knows where he's gone. . . ." She rose and went over to the other bed.

55

"I'm glad you took us with you," Ben said softly.

For a second Constance didn't respond. "I wish it had been to a different place than this," she said.

Tomorrow, Ben thought, Felice and I will prove to you that it wasn't a mistake for us to come. He lay awake in bed imagining how they would find their father: eating breakfast at a hotel coffee shop, or sitting behind a limousine in a chauffeur's uniform, or just driving down the street in his Pontiac, wearing his faded fishing cap. But whatever he was doing when Ben found him, his surprised father always greeted him with a gruff embrace.

The next morning Constance left the hotel a little before ten to resume her search with Randall, who had agreed to take her to some other employment agencies. As soon as she'd left, Ben started to dress. "If we're going to go, we'd better hurry," he told Felice.

"Where are we going, Ben?" Jube asked, sitting up in bed.

"To find some swings," Ben said. "You can't tell Momma, though. It's a secret."

"Oh, I like secrets," Jube said eagerly.

Before they left Ben shoved the suitcase with their money well under their bed and carefully locked the door to their room. Although he felt a little uneasy leaving their money unguarded, he knew it was safer hidden away in the room than it would be if he carried it with him on the streets.

Walking down the corridor they passed by the boy who had cut ahead of Ben and Jube at the bathroom. He was standing shirtless outside the shower, wearing his

Yankee cap and holding a towel. "Haven't they kicked you out yet?" he jeered.

Ben ignored him.

"The white trash they're letting in these days," the boy muttered loud enough for them to hear.

"What's 'white trash'?" Jube asked as they descended the stairs.

"Forget it," Ben told him. Soon they'd be leaving it all behind.

Outside the hotel they turned uptown, toward the city's gleaming office buildings, which seemed to catch all the rays of the early morning sun, shrouding the skid-row streets in shadows. As they moved toward the glittering, silvery towers, Ben felt his spirits begin to rise. He could sense the city of dreams that had lured his father to California. He was certain this was where they would find him.

They hurried past the bars and tiny liquor stores and markets, already open and doing business. The smell of fresh sugar doughnuts and coffee mingled with the stale smell of beer. They approached a burger-and-burrito stand, and the sizzle of grease, like a sharp blow to the stomach, reminded Ben just how little he had eaten in the last few days. The tangy odors had the same effect on Jube.

"I want a hamburg," he said, stopping in front of the stand.

"No money." Ben pulled him along.

"But my stomach's hungry," Jube protested, dragging his feet.

Felice grabbed his other arm. "Tell your stomach to go back to sleep," she said.

Another block and they turned down Broadway, a street bustling with people and traffic. There were dress shops, TV and stereo stores, movie theaters with Spanish and English films. The roar of buses and blare of horns mixed with the Mexican music playing in the record stores and the babble of languages on the street. Although a few men stood idly by the shops, with downcast or empty faces, most of the people were hurrying somewhere. Even the men collecting cans and garbage in their shopping carts looked more energetic here than they did on the streets near the Athens.

At the corner of Broadway and Fifth they stood for a few moments, listening to a street peddler hawk a windup monkey in Spanish and English. Across the street, by a newsstand, a blind guitar player sang hymns to collect money. Another street performer, a young ventriloquist, strolled along trying to engage people in conversation with his Howdy Doody dummy. The dummy, paint peeling from his nose, rolled his eyes at them as the ventriloquist passed by.

Somewhere, among these hundreds of people, could be my father, Ben thought. If we wait long enough on this corner, maybe he will walk by, too.

"Where are we going?" Jube asked.

Like a lost animal, Ben could only go on instinct. "That way," he said, pointing further uptown, in the direction of a castlelike turret that caught his eye. Taking Jube's hand, he led them across the street.

The tower two blocks away belonged to the Biltmore Hotel, a bright, brick building with a pillared entrance and canopied windows. The hotel was several times the size of the Athens and overlooked a small, grassy park that was ringed by small palm trees.

"They don't have swings here," Jube said disappointedly as they walked through the park, which was littered with people sleeping on the grass.

"It's not a park for children," Felice said, stepping around a man lying asleep against his backpack, snoring at the sky.

They stood gazing at the Biltmore, watching the tan-uniformed doorman help guests in and out of taxis and limousines.

"Let's go inside," Ben said.

"Do you think Daddy's really staying here?" Felice asked.

"I know it's pretty fancy," Ben said. He thought of the house on Stradella Road. "But maybe Daddy's working there. That could be, too."

They crossed the street and entered through the hotel's glass doors into an enormous courtyard with a fountain and potted palms and cut-glass chandeliers. The vaulted ceiling was several stories high and covered with painted wood beams.

"It's like a church," Jube exclaimed.

Only people were not praying but sitting around glass tables, in flowered chairs and sofas, drinking coffee and reading newspapers.

"How are we going to find out if he's here?" Felice asked.

Ben wasn't quite sure himself. In his worn jeans and thrift-shop jacket, he felt as out of place here as he had in Bel-Air. But if he found his father, none of it would matter. "There must be a place where you check in," he said. "We can ask there."

They walked through the courtyard, climbed a marble staircase with polished brass banisters, and passed through an ornate, gold-colored doorway sculpted with angels. The immense corridor in which they found themselves had large, colorful rugs. The ceilings were painted with what Ben imagined to be more angels, although he doubted that his Baptist minister in El Paso would've considered the naked women dancing and playing instruments proper pictures for his church. Felice and Jube stood gaping at the ceiling.

Seeing a uniformed bellboy carrying suitcases down the hallway, Ben tore his brother and sister away from the paintings and followed the bellboy to the lobby, a room almost as large as the El Paso bus station. A stone lion spit water from a fountain on the wall while well-dressed people sat in plush couches and chairs or waited to register at the front desk, which took up a whole end of the room.

"Are you going to ask?" Felice prodded him in a whisper that Ben was sure everyone in the lobby could hear.

"Wait here! And don't move!" he ordered, pushing her toward a flowered couch to keep her from calling any more attention to them. Then he turned and quickly stepped up to the desk.

"Can I help you?" a pretty young woman asked.

"I'm looking for . . . Clyde Gibson," he said, his mouth so dry he could barely get out the words.

The woman smiled and directed him to a phone across the room. "Dial the operator and she'll connect you."

"You mean he's here," Ben said excitedly.

"If he is, the operator will connect you," the woman said, turning to the man next to him in line.

Ben took a deep breath and strode across the room toward the phone. Despite his order to stay put, Felice and Jube both rose expectantly and followed him. "Is he really here?" Felice said incredulously. In answer Ben picked up the phone and dialed the hotel operator. "May I speak to Clyde Gibson," he said in a clear, firm voice, smiling at his sister.

In a few seconds the operator returned. "I'm sorry. There's no Gibson registered here."

Ben's hand tightened around the phone. "Are you sure? Could you tell me if he works here?"

"Just a moment and I'll check." There was a long pause before the operator returned. "I'm afraid there's no one named Gibson working here, sir."

"What? What?" Felice pressed as he hung up.

"He isn't here," Ben confessed. His face flushed with shame. How could he ever have let himself believe his father was staying in a place as grand as this?

Jube's eyes started to water. "Don't!" Ben grabbed his arm and squeezed. "Not here!" he pleaded. For Jube to start bawling now would be more humiliation than Ben could bear.

"C'mon," he urged, steering them toward the entrance to the street as Jube tried to sniff back his tears.

"Pardon please." A small Japanese man bowed in front of them. "I find this," he said, holding a ten-dollar bill in his hand.

Ben didn't understand what he was talking about.

"You leave on sofa," the man said in broken English, pointing to the couch where Felice and Jube had been sitting.

"Oh, thank you. Thank you very much," Felice said,

reaching for the money before Ben could tell the man it wasn't theirs.

"You welcome." The man smiled and bobbed his head again as he backed away.

Felice slipped the money in the pocket of her jeans and started for the entrance before anyone could discover the mistake. Ben and Jube hurried after her.

"That money wasn't yours," Ben said as soon as they got outside.

"The man thought it was," Felice countered.

"Because you lied to him."

"We need the ten dollars more than anybody staying at that hotel," Felice said hotly.

Although Ben didn't like lying, he couldn't argue with her. In fact, he wondered if that wasn't the reason the man had given them the money in the first place— because they looked like they needed it so badly.

"Can we get a hamburg now, Ben?" Jube asked.

"I guess so," he agreed. It was easier to spend the money than try to explain to their mother how they'd gotten it.

They walked back to the hamburger stand and ordered burgers and fries and milk shakes. Ben didn't know if it was the guilt for lying, or the disappointment of not finding his father, but he could barely touch the food. Untroubled by any remorse, Felice and Jube finished it for him.

Walking back to the hotel, Ben dropped fifty cents of their change into the cup of a legless man in a wheelchair. He knew it wouldn't make up for Felice's lie, but maybe it would keep them from being punished any further for their sins.

7

Halfway down the corridor, Ben saw that the door of their hotel room was open. His heart sank. His mother had gotten back before them.

When he reached the doorway, though, he discovered it was even worse. The lock had been forced or pried open and their suitcases and clothes were strewn about the room like garbage on the street.

Ben dived at the bag that had been under his bed and frantically searched for the sock in which his mother had hidden their money. Gone!

"The money!" he screamed at Felice and Jube. "Momma hid some money in a sock. Look for it!" But they cowered in the doorway, as though a rattlesnake were at their feet.

Desperately he attacked the second suitcase. Nothing! He picked it up in fury and dumped what was left inside it on the bed. Then he did the same thing to the other suitcase.

"Don't just stand there. Help me!" he yelled at his brother and sister.

Slowly they began picking up the clothes on the floor and bringing them over to the bed.

Ben sifted through each article and carefully repacked it in a suitcase. A useless effort. Locking the barn door after the horse had run away. The thief had broken in almost as easily as if Ben had left the key for him. It could have been anyone, a down-and-outer from the street who'd climbed up the fire escape, someone from the hotel who'd seen them leave, maybe even the skinhead manager.

"At least they didn't take Millie," Felice said, clutching her doll to her breast and rocking her back and forth.

"Who'd want to steal your dumb doll?" Ben sneered.

"Millie's not dumb," Felice protested. "She says we should never have left her alone."

"It was *your* idea to look uptown," he reminded her, sorry that he'd ever listened.

Felice was not about to take all the blame herself. "You thought Daddy was in that hotel. You said he was there. Didn't he, Jube?"

But Jube was too scared and confused to side with either of them. "Where's Momma?" he asked, curling around the pillow on his bed.

Ben had finished repacking the first suitcase and was sitting on the floor, finishing the second one, when Constance returned.

"What are you doing?" she asked in surprise.

Felice blurted it right out. "Somebody stole the money," she said. "They opened the suitcases and threw everything all over. . . ."

Constance looked down at Ben. He bowed his head.

"You left the room?" she said in disbelief.

He nodded, unable to meet her eyes.

"You knew the hotel wasn't safe. That lock was no better than a paper clip. . . ."

Ben couldn't think of anything to defend himself.

"All the money?" Constance said, slumping against the wall.

Not trusting himself to speak, Ben nodded again.

"I *told* you to stay here," she said. "I *counted* on you. . . . What were you thinking?"

He didn't see any way of explaining it to her.

"We went looking for Daddy," Felice confessed.

Constance ran her fingers through her hair in exasperation. "If you'd just done what I told you . . ."

Ben felt a sudden surge of anger. "We just wanted to help. You haven't found Daddy yet. Maybe you're not even looking in the right place. Following some man around who only met Daddy for a day . . ."

Her face hardened. "You know better, right? That's why our money's gone."

"We can't find Daddy by sitting here and praying," Ben said.

She looked at him with the same coldness with which she'd stepped around the drunk sprawled on the sidewalk. "Maybe your prayers aren't worthy enough for God to hear," she said.

Stung, Ben turned away. His cheeks burned as if she'd slapped him. God hasn't answered your prayers, either, he thought, but didn't say.

"Can we go back home now, Momma?" Felice asked timidly. She had clapped her hands over Millie's ears so that the doll could not hear the fighting.

Looking at Felice, Constance's eyes welled up with tears. "Not now, honey. I got less than twenty-five dollars left in my wallet. That money in the sock, that's what I was saving for bus fare in case we didn't find your daddy."

Ben couldn't stand to see his mother cry, to know how much he'd hurt her. He rose from the floor and grabbed his jacket and harmonica.

"I'll get it back for you," he said.

"Wait!" She reached out to stop him, but he slipped through her hands and out the door.

"Please, Ben, come back here. . . ." she called after him as he ran down the hall. He didn't look back.

Once outside, he headed straight for Broadway. He had seen enough street performers now to know exactly what to do. He found himself an unoccupied corner by a shoe shop, away from the blare of the stereo and TV stores, and put his jacket down on the sidewalk. To encourage people to contribute, he threw a few coins left from lunch on the jacket. Then he leaned against the building and began playing "The Worried Man Blues." People hurried by with hardly a glance. He switched to an upbeat tune. Maybe people will feel more generous if I can make them smile, he thought. Isn't a smile worth at least a quarter?

A few people seemed to think so. A mother pushing a baby in her stroller. A bearded young man with a camera, who asked if he could take his picture. A man with a shiny leather briefcase who asked him to play "I Wake Up with Heaven on My Mind." Since Ben didn't know the song, the man hummed it for him and Ben tried to play along. "Keep working at it, son." The man laughed and tossed two quarters at Ben's jacket.

Watching the people on the street, Ben tried to pick out the ones most likely to give him money and to catch their eye as they passed. Usually he didn't guess right. The fast-walking businessmen, the ones who looked as if they had plenty of change to spare, or the high-heeled women carrying fancy purses, rarely met his gaze or dropped a coin on his jacket. Sometimes, though, even they surprised him. One well-dressed man, who glanced irritably at Ben as he hurried by, turned abruptly a few yards down the street, came back, and handed him a dollar bill. Then he rushed off again before Ben could put his harmonica down and thank him.

Ben had no idea what had changed the man's mind. Maybe it was because he was playing "Old Folks at Home." Some people, he saw, liked it better when he played sad songs. If I looked raggedier and dirtier, he thought, they might give me even more money. Yet, like the businessman, when they did drop a coin in his jacket, they often looked embarrassed or resentful.

After an hour had passed on the shoe store clock, he took a break to count his money: three dollars and thirty-seven cents. His mouth was dry and his tongue sore, but he didn't feel quite as bad as when he'd fled the Athens. He knew now that he could make up for his mistake. In three or four days he could earn all the stolen money back. His mother would probably think of it as begging, and maybe it was, but her pride wouldn't feed them or pay for a hotel.

He wasn't the only person on the street who had swallowed his pride. The longer he stood on the corner, the more men—and women, too—he saw checking the trash baskets, searching for aluminum cans or anything else they might find. One of them was Nick.

Ben watched him dig through the concrete garbage barrel that had been picked clean several times before. He waited to see if Nick would say anything to him or pass by without a word.

Coming up empty, Nick pushed his grocery cart ahead and recognized Ben. He looked at him curiously, as if more puzzled than astonished to find him there, and leaned against his grocery cart, listening to Ben finish "Camptown Races."

"For a white boy, you don't play too bad," Nick said.

"Thanks," Ben said.

"But you don't know much about scuffling, do you, Tex?"

"What's scuffling?" Ben asked.

"What you doing, boy, hustling change, panhandling, trying to get by. . . ."

Ben reached into his pocket and pulled out some of his change. "I'm not doing so bad," he said.

Nick shrugged. "Maybe. But this corner be strictly low rent, if you know what I mean. You do a helluva lot better if you find yourself a more expensive piece of real estate."

"Like where?"

Nick paused. "You asking a lot for that quarter you threw me." He rubbed his bearded chin. "Don't you got no father to keep you off these streets?"

"He's not around right now," Ben answered.

Nick shook his head. "All right, follow the garbageman," he said, pushing his cart ahead.

Ben was a little surprised that Nick was being so friendly, but he decided to take a chance and tag along.

Scooping up the coins in his jacket, he followed Nick up the street as he moved from one trash basket to the next.

"Look at this, Tex. Look at this treasure." From a dumpster in front of an electronic discount store, Nick pulled out a twisted metal lamp that looked to Ben like someone had smashed it in a fit of anger. "I bet a story go with this," Nick said. He tossed it in his cart among the flattened beer and soda cans, the rags and discarded clothing.

"Never know what you going to find," he went on. "One man's rubbish be another's treasure." Nick found a soda can at last, dropped it on the sidewalk, and stomped on it as if it were a roach. He threw the prize into his cart.

"What do you do with all this stuff?" Ben asked.

"Sell it at the recycling depot. What do you think?"

"Can you make much money?"

"Do I look rich to you, boy?" Nick glared.

Ben decided not to press the question. There was a jitteriness to Nick that made Ben wary. He felt that at any moment Nick might turn on him with the same enthusiasm that he flattened cans.

They passed a pizza parlor and Nick checked the dumpster in the alley. He didn't find any leftovers to suit his taste. "Used to be a lot easier to get by down here," he said, moving on. "Some places they even wrapped the food they threw out. Now they be soaking it in bleach to keep bums like me from going through their trash. Afraid we going to scare away the customers." He made a menacing face that exposed his missing teeth.

Although Ben grinned at his scarecrow expression, he remembered how he'd felt the first time he saw Nick diving in the dumpster.

"It be getting worse all the time," Nick continued as they entered the park across from the Biltmore. "Look at you. How come a boy your age out scuffling?"

Ben told him about their money being stolen.

Nick shook his head as if Ben should have expected it. "You remember what I told you, boy. You don't trust nobody. You fall asleep in the park and you wake up with your pockets empty and your shoes gone. You got to keep awake all the time. People down here, they even steal the shoelaces off you."

Looking at Nick's cracked and dirt-caked shoes, Ben noticed, for the first time, that their laces were missing.

Nick found a cigarette butt in the grass and sat down on a bench to smoke it. Ben sat down with him, careful to keep a little distance between them.

"How come your momma brought you all the way up here from Texas?" Nick asked.

Ben told him how they'd come to find his father. "Maybe you've seen him," he said. "His name's Clyde Gibson." He described his father as carefully as he could.

"This is a big city, Tex. A lot of people in it. Why you think I'd know him?"

Ben looked down at his tennis shoes. "Sometimes he drinks a little," he said softly.

"Well, that be a different story, boy. If he only drinks a little, then he wouldn't be hanging 'round here. 'Cause the people I know in this neighborhood, hell, they all drink a lot."

He turned to a man with a swollen and discolored face sitting on the next bench. "Ain't that right, man?"

"Whatever you say, bro," the man answered, staring dully at the pigeons.

Ben couldn't tell whether Nick was laughing at him or not. "If my dad was down here," he said tentatively, "how could I find him?"

Nick finished his butt, rose, and hitched up his suspenders. "If a man want to hide down here, Tex, ain't nobody going to find him." He shoved his cart forward and they crossed the street to the Biltmore. A tour bus was unloading its passengers at the front door.

"Now we be getting into some high-class real estate," Nick said. "This ain't a good place to set up, though. The doorman just chase you away."

They turned away from the hotel and headed up another street. Nick continued sifting through the city's garbage baskets as they walked, but aside from a few cans, he found little to his liking.

"What about the missions?" Ben asked.

"What about them?" Nick said.

"Do you think my daddy could be at one of them?"

"That all depend on your daddy."

"Have you ever stayed at one?" Ben asked.

"Yeah, when it get cold enough down here, I stop in for a night. But I don't have no use for missions otherwise. I don't need nobody to look down their snooty noses at me to make me feel like scum." If that was the way they made you feel at the missions, Ben was sure his mother would never find his father there.

"In case you haven't figured it out yet, boy, there ain't no such thing as real charity. People don't give you no bed or food or money 'cause they want to help you out. They just do it to make themselves feel better or 'cause they don't want to see your ass anywhere near their door."

Ben thought of all the people who had given him money that morning. He couldn't believe that everyone was like that.

They crossed another street to a large bank building whose smoked glass windows made it impossible to see inside. Men and women passed in and out of the building like passengers on an escalator.

"You looking for money, you go where the banks are," Nick said. "Play that mouth organ here and see how you make out."

Ben felt more awkward and out of place here among the well-dressed and wealthy than he had on Broadway. He set his jacket down on the sidewalk nervously and took out his harmonica.

"You know 'We're in the Money Now'?" Nick flashed his gap-toothed grin.

Ben shook his head.

"Well, you better learn it, son." He turned and steered his grocery cart down the street.

"Thanks," Ben called after him, but Nick didn't look back.

Three hours later Ben returned to the hotel with almost sixteen dollars in his pocket. He had barely knocked on the door of his family's room when Felice threw it open. "I knew you'd come back," she exclaimed.

"Oh, Ben," Constance said, rising from the bed. "You had us worried sick. . . ."

Ben reached into his pockets and threw the coins he had collected on the bed. "It's not much," he said, "but I can get more tomorrow."

Constance recoiled from the money as if it had been stolen. "Where did you get this?" she said.

Ben pulled out his harmonica. "Working," he said.

"You don't have to earn it back, son. We'll find a way to get by. We got our room paid until Monday. . . ." She came over and enfolded him in her arms. "I didn't mean what I said before. It was my fault, not yours. I should've known better than to leave the money in the suitcase. . . ."

Ben stood there stiffly as she went on berating herself. No matter how hard he tried, it seemed he still couldn't make things right.

8

It began raining on Friday morning and continued, on and off, through the weekend. The water quickly soaked through the cardboard window patch and formed a large puddle in the corner of the Gibsons' room. By Saturday the rain was also dripping from several places in the ceiling, one directly over Ben and Jube's bed. Constance went downstairs and complained to the desk clerk. When she returned to the room, Ben saw her face was tight with anger. The clerk had shrugged and told his mother to move the bed. Since they had no money to move elsewhere, there was little else they could do. Constance was having difficulty enough finding them a place to stay when their week ran out at the hotel.

Another woman at the Athens had told Ben's mother about the city's emergency shelters and, beginning Friday morning, she spent many hours—and even more quarters of their dwindling cash—on the pay telephone in the hotel's seedy lobby. The problem, she explained to Ben, was that only a few of the shelters were for families. And although she telephoned them every day, none of them had vacant beds.

Ben tried to convince his mother to let him earn their room money by playing his harmonica on the streets, but she wouldn't hear of it. "I won't have my family begging," she said.

"It's not begging. It's entertaining," Ben argued. "Lots of people do it."

"Not my family," she said firmly. "We've never had to live off charity before."

"Isn't staying at a shelter taking charity, too?" Felice asked.

"In a way I suppose you could say that," Constance said, "but I'd call it Christian kindness myself."

"What if no shelter will take us?" Felice worried.

"The Lord won't let little children sleep in the streets," her mother assured her.

Ben was not so sure about the Lord, but he knew his mother's pride would keep them from sleeping in doorways. When his father couldn't get work, she had found a job herself to keep their family from going on welfare. Now she was even reluctant to spend the sixteen dollars Ben had earned with his harmonica. Only when they'd finished all the canned goods Randall had given them, and the last dollar bill in her purse was gone, did she break down and use some of the money to buy food. No matter what her reservations about begging, she couldn't let them go hungry.

The day before they had to leave the hotel, she also found them a place to stay—the Heavenly Light Mission.

"It's a church several miles from downtown that never turns anyone away," she explained, adding, "I don't know what it's going to be like."

"It can't be worse than here," Felice grumbled. The rain had forced them to stay inside the damp hotel room with little to do all weekend but play cards and get on each other's nerves. To add to everyone's irritability, Jube had come down with a cold on Saturday and had been dripping and sniffling over everything ever since.

They were all happy to pack their bags on Monday morning and leave the Athens. Because the mission was too far to walk and difficult to reach by bus, Randall offered to drive them there. Though Constance hadn't seen him since Thursday, she spoke to him on the phone each day. Ben didn't understand why his mother trusted Randall so much. The only real help he'd provided so far had been the can opener and a few groceries.

As the Gibsons waited inside the hotel lobby, the youth with the backward baseball cap walked in the front door. He took in their suitcases with surprise. "You leaving this flea trap?" He seemed disappointed to discover it.

Ben didn't answer. Since the theft of their money, he regarded everyone in the hotel as a possible thief. And this boy in particular.

"Yes, we're moving on," Constance answered pleasantly.

"To Bel-Air," Ben jumped in, "where all the rich people live."

The boy looked as astonished as Constance and Felice. "Well, lucky you," he said in a sneering tone.

"Better be real good, or else they'll be sending you right back here." He kicked over one of their suitcases as he shoved past and climbed the stairs.

Ben picked up the bag. "Did that boy do something to you?" Constance asked.

"He's mean," Jube said, clinging to his mother with one hand and wiping his runny nose with the other.

"Living at this hotel a long time could make anybody mean," Constance said.

A horn honked as a beat-up old Chevrolet Impala pulled up in front of the hotel. "That's him," said Constance.

A tall man with thinning hair got out of the car. Even though the day was cloudy, he wore dark sunglasses. As he walked slowly toward the hotel, Ben noticed he had a limp.

"This here's Randall," Constance shyly introduced him.

Ben put down his suitcase and stuck his hand out to greet him.

"Your momma's told me a lot about you kids," Randall said. His hand was rough and callused, his clothes as worn as the paint on his dented Chevy.

Ben quickly glanced at his sister to see her reaction. From the way she hugged Millie, he knew exactly what she was thinking: Randall looked like he needed help more than they did.

Ben got in the backseat with Felice while Constance and Jube sat in the front with Randall. The car's upholstery was all torn up and there was a gaping hole in the dashboard where the radio should have been. The engine clunked and sputtered.

Ben thought of his father's Pontiac. Even after he'd lost his job, he'd always managed to keep the GTO clean and shiny.

Randall drove them several miles from downtown to an area of the city they had never been before. Graffiti-scrawled, stucco cottages shared the streets with old, two-story wooden houses that had fallen on hard times. Their front porches were sagging, their yards dried up or gone to weeds. Only the palm trees that rose high above the broken-down houses seemed untouched by the general decay.

The Heavenly Light Mission was located on a dead-end street, walled off from the freeway by a thick barrier of concrete. The wooden church didn't look any better off to Ben than the rest of the neighborhood. Its white paint was peeling and its frosted yellow windows all had protective gratings. The mission's only adornment was a small electric cross that topped its simple wooden steeple, but the cross wasn't turned on in the daylight.

Randall pulled his car up in front of the church and cut the engine. "I guess this is it," he said. They sat there a moment watching some small children chase a mangy dog through the parking lot.

"Well, at least you'll have some other kids to play with," Constance said.

"Where do you sleep?" Felice asked the same question Ben was thinking. The church was smaller than the one they attended in El Paso.

"Well, we can't find out sitting here," Randall said, opening his door.

They walked up the steps and entered the mission. The inside was as plain as the exterior and smelled of a lemony deodorizer. There were two offices at the front of the church, both closed, and a large bulletin board of photographs and notices. The chapel took up the rest of the building. Women stood talking in the aisles or sitting in the wooden pews watching a color television on the altar. Several barefooted children played on the thinly carpeted floor or crawled over the seats. No one came up to greet the Gibsons.

"The beds must be downstairs," Ben said.

The ground floor contained no sleeping accommodations though, either, only a men's and women's bathroom, a small kitchen with two padlocked refrigerators, and a large dining room with long metal tables and folding chairs.

"Looks like you sleep in the seats upstairs," Randall said, "same as the missions."

Constance looked around, disheartened. "I guess that's why they have room for everybody," she said.

"Like I said before, you're welcome to stay at my place," Randall offered.

Ben glanced at his mother in surprise. She hadn't said a word to them about Randall's invitation.

"Thanks," Constance said, "but you've done enough already."

"I'm not doing it as a favor," Randall said. "I'd like you to come."

Constance flushed with embarrassment. "I'm sure we'll be fine here," she said.

"Suit yourself," Randall said curtly and limped outside to get their bags.

Jube tugged at his mother's sleeve. "I don't feel so good," he said between sniffles.

"I know, honey, I know," Constance said soothingly.

79

"In just a little bit we'll find a place for you to lie down."

She led them back upstairs to the offices. This time one of the doors was open. A small, gray-haired woman emerged with a teenage girl who cradled a squalling baby in her arms. "There, there, everything's going to be all right now," the girl kept repeating as she tried to quiet her baby, but from her own reddened eyes, Ben wasn't sure if she really believed it.

After helping the girl to a bench, the older woman returned to the Gibsons and introduced herself as the pastor's wife. She welcomed them to the mission and said they could stay there as long as they were in need. Then she gave Constance some forms to fill out and a list of rules and regulations. The church, she quickly explained, would feed them three meals a day and give them blankets to sleep on the floor. In return they were expected to help with the chores, spend an hour and a half reading the Bible each morning, and attend a prayer service each night. And if they stayed at the shelter longer than a week, Ben and Felice would have to attend the local schools.

"We sure 'preciate this," Constance said with far more gratitude than Ben felt.

"We provide as the Lord makes possible for each one He sends to our door," the woman said mechanically. Ben wondered how many times she repeated the same words each day.

When Randall brought in their bags, the crying baby had been joined by two other screaming infants in the church. Randall shook his head at the noise. "If you change your mind, you know how to reach me," he told Constance.

"Why can't we stay with him?" Felice whispered to Ben as Constance walked Randall to the door.

Ben wasn't sure himself. Although he hadn't particularly liked what he'd seen of Randall, he didn't see how staying at his place could be worse than sleeping on the floor with dozens of strangers and crying babies.

"I guess Momma doesn't know him well enough," he said.

"We don't know these people, either," Felice said in disgust.

By five-thirty the shelter looked like a fast-food restaurant on Broadway. The lines of people waiting for their dinner stretched from the serving counter to the door at the opposite end of the concrete-floored dining hall. Although some of the people looked as down and out as skid-row drunks, most of them looked no different than the families Ben had seen eating at McDonald's.

Downtown he'd seen few children. Here there were dozens of them, although most younger than he. That afternoon he and Felice had sat out on the back steps of the church watching them return from school. It wasn't long before some girls invited Felice to jump rope with them. Ben joined some younger boys tossing a football around for a while, but he preferred sitting on the steps and observing the residents of the shelter. People stood in small groups in the parking lot, speaking in different accents, and even different languages. Ben tried to imagine where all of them had come from or what bad luck had brought them to the shelter. Whatever their story, the presence of so many other homeless families made him feel a little less ashamed to be there.

The shelter, though, only seemed to discourage his mother more. Lining up for dinner, she stood with downcast eyes, holding on to Jube's hand. When they received their food, she sat them as far away as possible from everyone else at the table. And even though the two hot dogs and noodles were the first hot meal they'd eaten in days, Constance only finished half of it, dividing the rest among her children. Ben could tell that Jube was really feeling sick when he turned down his second helping.

As they were finishing their meal, a tall, slender man asked Constance if she minded if he and his son sat next to them. Constance shook her head and they sat down beside her.

Ben guessed the boy was three or four years older than he and was almost as tall as his father. He must have shot up only recently for his denim jacket ended several inches above his bony wrists.

"You're new here, aren't you?" the man asked.

Constance told him that they'd just arrived that day. "You been here long?" she asked.

"Since Thursday," he said.

"But we're leaving first thing Saturday morning," the boy said, looking at his father. "First thing."

The father confirmed it. "We're just waiting till we collect our paychecks."

Ben asked where they were going.

"Away from here," the boy said emphatically.

"Everything costs more here than Saint Louis," the father said uncomfortably. "The money we had didn't stretch as far as we expected. . . ."

Constance nodded with sympathy. It was all the encouragement the man needed. His story tumbled out like a long blues rift on the harmonica. After a year's illness his wife had died of cancer the previous November. During her final months, he had taken a leave from his job at a furniture factory to nurse her, and between her medical bills and his not working, he had used up all their savings. While he was caring for his wife the furniture factory hired someone else to replace him, and when he fell too far behind on his mortgage payments, the bank foreclosed on his house. As he told all this, he ran his hand up and down the sleeve of his son's denim jacket. "In a year I lost everything," he said. "Everything except my boy."

He paused and rested his hand on his son's shoulder. "I don't know what I would've done without him," he said.

The boy stopped eating a moment to smile at his father, then continued their story. "So last month we sold about everything we owned except our truck and drove out here to start over again. It took longer than we thought to get work, but we finally got ourselves a job roofing. This Friday we pick up our first paychecks," he said proudly.

"It's a blessing that they have places like this to help you out when you're in need," the father said.

The boy jabbed his fork into his hot dog. "It's no blessing to be here." He turned to Ben. "You know a lot of people stay here months, even a year, living like this. . . ."

"It does eat away at your pride," the father admitted. "You got to get out as soon as you can, before you get trapped here." He looked directly at Constance. "Not just for your sake, but your kids' sake."

"I 'preciate what you're saying," Constance said.

"I could tell you're the kind of woman who would," the father said kindly. "Remind me a little of my wife." He looked away a moment, then quickly bent his head over his food.

That night, at the evening prayer service, Ben thought about the boy and his father while the pastor droned on about "the sins of America." Despite the loss and hardships the family from Saint Louis had suffered, Ben couldn't help envying them a little. He kept remembering the way the father looked at his son.

He hoped his mother would follow their advice and leave the shelter quickly. Though earlier it had eased his shame to discover that so many others shared his family's problems, he found he didn't like waiting in line with them for dinner or the bathroom, or sitting at the evening service in an overheated room of unwashed bodies. Ben would've liked to have taken a shower himself, but with only one at the shelter, you had to sign up three or four days in advance.

As Ben listened to the minister ramble on and on about "what a fearful thing it is to fall into the hands of a living God," he tried to figure out where all the people sitting in the crowded pews were going to sleep that night. He counted 167 people at the service, give or take a few squirming children who kept popping up and down in their mother's laps. The longer the minister went on, the more restless everyone became. Even his mother, Ben noticed, wasn't paying much attention to the minister's sermon. Not once did she join the feeble chorus of "Amens" and "Praise the Lords" that the congregation occasionally uttered.

Finally the minister finished. Most of the churches in America, he concluded, didn't want to have anything to do with the poor. They were only looking for "the healthy, wealthy, and wise." But Christ, he reminded them, had embraced "the poor, the sick, the fallen, and the homeless." And so did the Heavenly Light Mission. For as Jesus had said, " 'Blessed are the poor in spirit: for theirs is the kingdom of heaven.' "

Heaven is a long time to wait to receive God's blessing, Ben thought as he bowed his head with the rest of the congregation. If God really loves all His children, as the minister says, why does He let so many of them live this way?

When the service was over, people began to collect their blankets and get ready for the night. The people who had been there before had already staked out their pews or places on the floor. When newcomers tried to claim their bed sites, tempers flared, and men and women swore and shouted at each other. The man from Saint Louis helped Constance find a spot on the floor between some back-row pews where the Gibsons could all squeeze in together. Since there was no place to change for the night except the bathrooms, and there was a line stretching up the stairs to get in, Ben's family, like most people, chose to sleep in their clothes. When the church lights dimmed at nine, though, some children, and even a few adults began stripping to their underwear. Constance quickly made Ben and Felice lie on the floor so they could not watch.

The space between the pews was so cramped Ben could barely move without disturbing everyone else sleeping in that row. The carpeting was thin and didn't provide much padding. Ben tried sleeping on his back at first, but looking up at the seats, he saw roaches crawling not more than a foot above him. He turned over and pulled the thin blanket over his head, hoping that Felice, who lay on her stomach beside him clutching Millie, wouldn't roll over, open her eyes, and start screaming.

Throughout the church babies were fussing and crying. On the other side of him, Jube curled up under Constance's blanket, coughed and wheezed. Outside Ben could hear the cars whizzing past on the freeway, people probably heading home to their warm beds.

He felt a surge of anger rising in his chest. "How can God let people live like this?" he whispered to his mother.

She was lying so close to him on the floor that even in the dim light he could see the tears in her eyes as she turned to him. "Don't blame God for this," she said softly. "This is an embarrassment to Him, too."

9

When they turned the church lights on again at five-thirty Tuesday morning, Jube was coughing so hard that he could barely catch his breath.

"Jube looks real bad, Momma," Felice said, alarmed.

"I know," Constance said. Her own face was paler than the morning light. Ben figured she'd been up most of the night with Jube.

"What are we going to do?" Felice asked.

"We got to find somewhere else to stay. The floor's no place for a sick child."

"It's no place for anyone," Ben said. He'd only been able to sleep for a few hours himself.

Before breakfast was served at eight, there was an hour and a half of required Bible reading and prayer. Bibles were passed out to those who didn't have any, including children old enough to read. Ben opened his book to a random page but couldn't bring himself to study it. Felice, and a number of other people, sat in the pews and fell back to sleep. Though Constance stared at her Bible, Ben didn't see her turn a page.

The breakfast of cold scrambled eggs and butterless

toast was small reward for the morning's prayer. The food had no taste and didn't fill Ben's stomach.

The pastor's wife, walking through the dining room, saw Jube coughing and came over to Constance. "That child needs to be looked at by the nurse," she scolded. "We don't want him infecting everyone around here." She told Constance that the nurse came to the church every morning after breakfast and that Constance should take Jube right upstairs to wait for her.

Either the mention of the nurse or the woman's tone frightened Jube, for tears welled up in his eyes like liquid in a straw.

Felice put her arm around her little brother. "It's not anyone's fault that Jubie's sick," she said, smarting at the way the pastor's wife had spoken to Constance.

"That woman has a lot more people to think of than us," Constance said. "It's good they have a nurse here."

Judging from the line that formed outside the office where the nurse examined patients, the shelter was not a very healthy place. There were other children who were wheezing and coughing as bad as Jube. One mother held a wiggly two-year-old in an effort to keep him from scratching the ugly red sores on his legs. Another little girl with a bandage on her arm clung tearfully to her mother.

Ben and Felice went back downstairs and waited outside the church while Constance joined the unhappy line. After about an hour Constance came out to get them. Jube was sucking a lollipop.

"She gave me some medicine," Jube said, looking pleased with himself despite his pale face and bleary eyes.

"The nurse gave him some aspirin and cough medicine," Constance explained, "but she said it won't do much good unless he gets some rest."

"Where's he going to get that?" Ben asked.

"I've called Randall," Constance said. "He's coming in a while to pick us up."

She looked tired and defeated as she gazed past them at the wall that separated them from the freeway. Ben was sure she was regretting that they'd left El Paso.

Randall lived in a different section of Los Angeles than the mission, but his neighborhood was no better. His apartment was one of a motel-like cluster of crumbling stucco cottages a few miles south of downtown. An old Ford with a smashed windshield sat abandoned in the front yard on flattened tires.

The inside of the cottage was dank and gloomy and had a faint, moldy smell of spoiled food. The living room rug was much more worn than the one at the church and the furniture was as broken-down as the dresser in the Athens. Besides the living room, there was a bedroom with a wooden crucifix above the bed, a small kitchen area with a grease-encrusted stove, and a bathroom with a tub and leaky toilet.

"It's not much," Randall apologized, "but you can stay here till you find better."

Ben felt his stomach shrivel up as he looked around the cottage. He wondered if the reason Randall kept his sunglasses on was to avoid noticing how miserable a place it was.

Randall did have a bed, though, and Constance immediately put Jube in it to sleep. "I'm kind of worn down myself," she said, lying down beside him. Within minutes they were both asleep.

Randall closed the bedroom door to keep from disturbing them. He had an old television set in the living room and turned it on low for Felice and Ben. The picture was black-and-white and fuzzy.

Felice got up and fiddled with the dial. "How do you get the color?" she asked.

"You got to add it. In your head," Randall said. "It's much better that way. You can make things whatever color you want."

Felice didn't think his joke was very funny. She snapped the dial impatiently trying to find something to watch.

"Careful you don't break it," Randall warned.

Felice gave him a sour look and settled on an old Three Stooges show. She plopped down on the torn sofa to amuse herself. Ben had no interest in the TV. He wanted to find out from Randall about his father.

He went over to the table where Randall was making himself a cup of instant coffee. "Where did you meet my dad?" Ben asked.

"At that job center," Randall said, tasting his coffee. Not finding it to his liking, he dumped in more sugar from the box.

"You go there a lot?" Ben continued.

"Sometimes, when my leg's not acting up."

"What happened to your leg?" Felice, who had been listening from the couch, dared to ask.

Randall peered at her from behind his dark glasses. "It got shot up, in 'Nam."

"Oh." Felice gulped. She rose and came over to the table. "What's a Nam?" she asked.

"It's short for Vietnam," Randall explained, "a rotten country far away from here."

Ben didn't really care how Randall hurt his leg. "Did you and Daddy get to be friends?" he asked.

Randall took another drink of his coffee and considered the question. "Yeah, we hung together a couple of days," he said, sitting at the table.

"Did he say anything about us?" Ben asked.

"I don't recall he did," Randall replied. "He didn't strike me as the family type. First I knew he had kids was when I met your mother."

Ben didn't believe his father had forgotten them that quickly. "Momma said you told her Daddy might be staying at the missions," Ben went on. "But why would he go there when he could sleep in his car?"

Randall frowned. "He didn't have any car that I saw."

"Do you know what happened to it?" Ben said casually.

Randall's eyes were masked behind his sunglasses. "He didn't say."

Ben glanced at Felice. Could she see that Randall couldn't have spent much time with their father?

"He talk at all about fishing?" Ben continued.

"What difference does it make what he talked about?" Randall said testily.

Now Ben was certain. Either Randall had never met his father, or if he had, he certainly hadn't been his friend.

Felice knew it, too. "Daddy always talks about fishing," she boldly challenged Randall.

"Well, not to me," he said, setting his coffee cup down hard on the table. "Why don't you kids go out and play? The fresh air'll do you good."

Felice sniffed the air dramatically. "It sure will," she said.

The muscles tensed in Randall's jaw. "Do it, then!" He picked up the newspaper and dismissed them.

"He doesn't know Daddy," Ben said as soon as they were outside.

"Then why did he tell Momma that he did?"

Ben couldn't answer her. He was surprised his mother hadn't seen through Randall's lies herself. Hadn't she asked him any of these questions?

"We got to tell her," Felice said.

Ben agreed. If his mother counted on Randall for help, they would never find Clyde. They were, in fact, no closer to locating him now than they were when they'd arrived in Los Angeles. Since the theft of their money, Constance had barely had time to look for him, and the vagueness of her future plans worried Ben. "We're going to have to look for Daddy ourselves," he said.

"How are we going to do that?" Felice demanded.

Ben didn't have the answer to that yet, either. "We'll just have to find a way," he said.

"We'd better," Felice said, "because I sure don't want to stay here with Randall."

Ben didn't have an opportunity to talk with his mother until that evening when Randall went next door to see if he could find some juice for Jube.

"I don't think he knows Daddy." Ben related his fears.

His doubts did not persuade his mother. "How do you know what your daddy did or didn't say to him?" she said. "Whatever kind of friends they were, Randall's sure putting himself out for us."

Though Ben couldn't deny that, it didn't ease his suspicions. "How come he never takes his sunglasses off?" he asked.

" 'Cause of the medicine he takes. The light hurts his eyes," she explained.

"Medicine for his leg?"

Constance glanced at the front door as if she were afraid Randall might be listening outside. "The war was very hard on him," she said. "He's just now getting over it."

"Well, Millie doesn't like him," Felice said flatly. "She thinks he's mean."

"You hush up," Constance ordered. "He's doing his best, trying to help us out. He's just not used to having kids around. . . ."

Maybe she has to like him, Ben thought, because she doesn't know where else to turn. Still, he didn't see much to recommend Randall. A bad leg and bad nerves. A junk car and worse apartment. Whatever problems his father had, he had it all over Randall.

Randall returned with the juice, and he and Constance cooked up some soup and the few vegetables in Randall's refrigerator. Jube had slept almost all day and was feeling a little better now, but both Ben and Felice were exhausted from the previous night.

Although Randall offered to let Constance and Jube use his bed, Constance refused, saying that Jube was well enough to sleep on the couch. She and Ben and Felice would spend the night on the floor as they had at the mission. Here, at least, they would have room to sprawl out.

Having napped that afternoon with Jube, Constance

did not come to bed with them at once, but stayed up watching television in Randall's bedroom, where he had moved the set so that it wouldn't keep them awake. Tonight, neither the noise of the TV nor even the hard floor made any difference to Ben. Exhausted, he immediately fell asleep.

Sometime later, he was awakened by a noise in the kitchen. He raised his head to see Randall getting a can of soda from the refrigerator. The noise appeared to wake Felice as well for she stirred beside Ben. Randall must have thought they were still asleep, though, for he paid no attention to them as he returned to the bedroom with his soda.

Through the half-open door of the bedroom, Ben could hear his mother and Randall talking as they watched TV.

"You want to know what I really think?" Randall said, apparently continuing a conversation they had started earlier. "I think he's miles away from here. Portland. Seattle. Maybe even Alaska. It don't matter, really. Wherever he is, he don't want you with him."

Ben felt everything tense inside him. Were they talking about his father?

Constance's reply was too low to hear. But Randall seemed to be just warming up. "You got to face it," he said. "He's not coming back. Good riddance to bad rubbish, I say. You deserve a whole lot better. . . ."

Ben waited for his mother to object. If she did, her voice was lost in the music of a commercial.

"We've both had rotten breaks," Randall went on. "Bum husband, bum leg. A lot of pain. A lot of pain . . . If we joined up, maybe we could put all that behind us. A fresh start. For both of us . . ."

94

From his position on the floor, Ben could see Randall pacing the bedroom with excitement, dragging his game leg behind him.

"We could get you on welfare—if you got the right papers, it's only a few weeks wait—then we could pool our checks. Together we'd have enough to start over. I got about five hundred stashed away. Four or five hundred more and we'd have enough to put down first and last month's rent on someplace decent. Away from here. Where you don't look out the window at junked cars and winos sleeping on your doorstep . . ."

"A place where there's a good school for the kids," Constance said, her voice rising with hope.

Randall stopped his pacing. "I know how much you care about your kids, Connie. They're good kids, too, and you've been a good mother to them . . . but . . . well, the kids could be a problem right now. It's hard to get back on your feet with the three of them always under foot. It's not so easy to find a good place for five. . . ."

On the floor beside him, Felice reached over and clutched Ben's arm.

"I know it's not easy," Constance said.

"I don't want you to take this wrong," Randall said, "but with all the problems you got right now, maybe they'd be better off if you put them in a foster home awhile. . . ."

Ben held his breath.

"I couldn't do that," Constance protested. "I didn't come all this way to give up my children."

"I know that," Randall assured her. "Hear me out, will you. They wouldn't have to be away from you long, just till we worked things out, got back on our feet again. You want the best for your kids, don't you? Well, they sure can't get it living here. You want someplace safe for them, where you don't have to worry about drunks, and thieves, and addicts, where they can get three square meals a day and go to a good school. You can't give that to them now. Neither of us can. Once we get things settled, though . . ."

"There has to be another way. . . ." Constance's voice wavered. "I've been doing the best I know how. . . ."

"Don't I know that?" Randall said soothingly. "You're a good mother, Connie, a real good mother. . . ."

Ben couldn't be sure with the noise from the television set, but it sounded as if his mother was crying.

". . . That's why you want what's best for them," Randall went on. "That's why it's so hard. . . ."

"Don't. Don't say any more. *Please* . . ."

"Sure. I didn't mean to upset you. . . ." Ben saw Randall perch, like a vulture, on the far corner of the bed.

Ben turned to Felice in the darkness. "I'll run away before they split us up," he whispered to her fiercely. "I'll run away and find Daddy and come back for you and Jube."

10

Waking the next morning and finding his mother asleep beside him on the floor, Ben thought for a moment that he had dreamed the conversation of the night before. Constance was lying on her side facing him, her head resting on a makeshift pillow of clothes. With the tightness around her mouth relaxed by sleep, her usually careworn face was almost beautiful in the slash of light from the window. Could she really be thinking of sending them to foster homes?

She opened her eyes and discovered him sitting up, cross-legged, staring at her. "What's wrong?" she asked, startled.

"Nothing. Nothing's wrong," he said, not yet ready to confront her with what he'd overheard. He rose and headed for the bathroom.

Standing at the sink he splashed cold water on his face. He knew he had to think this out carefully. If his mother couldn't find a way to keep the family together, then he would have to find one himself. Nick had told the truth. You couldn't count on anyone but yourself.

At breakfast Ben watched his mother and Randall closely for clues to what they might be planning. Randall seemed in unusually good spirits, whistling as he limped around the kitchen making coffee for himself and Constance. "It's good to have company for breakfast," he said, smiling at Constance.

She smiled weakly back. Maybe, Ben hoped, she's having second thoughts about giving us up.

"When are we going to start looking for Daddy again?" he asked.

"I was thinking about going out for a little while this morning," she said.

Felice asked if they could go with her, but Constance wanted them to stay at the apartment with Jube. "I don't want to risk your brother's getting sick all over again," Constance said. "Besides, I'll only be gone a few hours."

"Where you going to look?" Ben asked casually.

"We're going to try welfare," Randall said.

Just as they planned last night, Ben thought bitterly. He couldn't believe his mother was actually going through with it.

"How can welfare help find Daddy?" he asked.

Constance looked uneasy. "If he applied for relief, they'll have records of it."

"Daddy doesn't like taking charity, either," Ben reminded her.

"The way I see it, it's not charity," Randall said, "and the way they give it out sure doesn't make you feel very grateful. When the government needed my help, I put in my time. They're not giving me anything now I didn't earn."

"Is that why you don't work?" Ben asked him.

"I work," Randall said testily, "when my leg's not bothering me and when there's a job to be had. But not many people are looking to hire guys like me."

Ben didn't care if no one would ever hire him. It still didn't excuse what he was trying to force Constance to do.

"Daddy didn't go on welfare in Texas, and I don't think he's gone on welfare here," Ben said, looking directly at his mother.

Constance began to clear the breakfast dishes. "We'll find out soon enough," she mumbled.

Ben waited until she went to the bathroom to dress and Randall was in the bedroom, then grabbed his mother's purse and took back some change and two of the seven remaining dollars from the money he'd earned on the street. Felice watched nervously, keeping one eye on the bedroom door to make sure Randall didn't walk out and catch him.

"Do you think Momma's really going to do it?" she asked after Constance and Randall had left the apartment.

"Why else would she be going to welfare?" Ben asked.

"What's Momma going to do?" Jube wanted to know.

"Nothing. It's none of your business," Felice flared up at him.

Jube looked fearfully at Ben. Ben knelt and put his hands on his brother's shoulders. "Look, can you keep a secret? It's very important."

Jube wiped his nose and nodded gravely.

"I have to go out for a while," Ben said, "to see if I can get us out of here. But I don't want Momma to know

99

about it. So you can't say anything to her when she comes back. You understand?"

Jube slowly shook his head yes.

"You'd better not say anything," Felice warned menacingly. "And you'd better be good while Ben is gone."

"I will," Jube said sullenly.

"If Momma gets back before I do, just tell her I went out for a walk," Ben said to his sister as she walked him to the door.

"Where are you going to go?" Felice asked.

"I'll tell you when I get back," he said, slipping out before she could press him any more. He was afraid that she wouldn't think much of what he had in mind.

At the street he turned back to see Felice and Jube watching him from the doorway, trusting that somehow he would find a way to rescue their family. He hoped he would not disappoint them.

The bus stop was only two blocks away, and within a few minutes a bus, headed downtown, stopped to pick him up. Ben got off on the same street as the Greyhound bus station and set off to find Nick. He wasn't really sure if Nick could help, but he didn't know anyone else to turn to. He headed toward the boarded-up pawnshop where he and Felice had seen Nick hanging out with his buddies.

The streets were crowded again this morning with men and women carrying their homes in shopping carts, a few of them already sifting through the morning garbage. On one street Ben passed a small line of men waiting in front of a storefront he had not noticed before. The sign in the window said EARN CA$H FOR YOUR BLOOD. Some of the men in line looked so sickly that Ben wondered how they could give away any blood at all. Further down the street, two well-dressed young men huddled in a doorway flashing rolls of bills and exchanging merchandise. Drugs, Ben guessed. He hurried on toward the pawnshop.

Today only the scar-faced man and a heavyset man on crutches were drinking their breakfast in the doorway. Remembering his last encounter with the scar-faced man, Ben slowed down. He stopped several feet from the doorway, trying to fight off the fear knotting in his chest.

"Do you know where Nick is?" he asked in a voice barely louder than the traffic.

The scar-faced man looked at him without recognition. "What'd you say?"

"Nick. I'm looking for Nick," Ben said a little more distinctly.

"What d'you want Nick for?" His scar stood out like a red neon light on his gray flesh.

"I need to talk to him."

"What for?" He passed the bottle to his friend.

"I just do."

"Well, he can't be disturbed now," Scarface said.

"Yeah, he's out doing salvage work." The heavyset man laughed and wiped the mouth of the bottle with a dirty hand before he took a drink.

"You can talk to us," Scarface offered. "We're just as good as Nick. What do you need him for?"

Ben knew that if he tried to explain they'd only give him a harder time. "Has he been by here this morning?" he asked.

"How bad do you want to find Nick?" Scarface said.

"What do you mean?" Ben asked shakily.

"He means bad enough to pay." The man on crutches chuckled.

"Is it worth a dollar to you?" Scarface asked.

"I don't have a dollar."

"How about a quarter?"

Ben fingered the few coins in his pocket. "I don't have a quarter, either," he said, growing angry.

"What do you have in them pockets?" Scarface asked.

Ben held up a dime. "That's all I got. But I'll give it to you to find out."

"A dime ain't worth it," Scarface said, taking another drink.

Angrily Ben shoved the coin back into his pocket. This was just a game to them. "I'll find him myself," he said, and turned away.

"Wait a minute, kid," the man on crutches called after him. "I'll tell you for a dime."

The scar-faced man drained the wine bottle and flung it against the wall in disgust. "Save your money, kid. He don't know where Nick is anymore than I do."

The man on crutches stuck out a swollen, dirty hand. "Is it worth a dime to find out?"

Ben grabbed the coin from his pocket and stuck it in the man's greedy palm.

"The Harmony Camp," the man said, "that's where he's sleeping these days. In one of those cardboard con-dos . . ."

He gave Ben directions and Ben took off in relief. In five minutes he reached the camp of sidewalk squatters.

A shantytown had been set up on both sides of the street: tents, lean-tos draped with plastic tarpaulins and blankets, cardboard boxes and makeshift wooden shelters. There were even two portable toilets, one on either side of the street. People sat out on a jumble of old furniture and shopping carts playing cards and dominoes or cooking over gasoline-can stoves. The smell of stew mingled with the acrid smoke of plastic food containers and worn-out clothes that stoked the fires.

The camp and its inhabitants took up so much of the sidewalk that Ben had to walk in the street. He strolled past the different dwellings, looking for Nick. The residents of the camp had tried their best to make their impoverished living quarters look like real homes. A few people had placed rug remnants in front of their tents like welcome mats. Another couple had put up flowered curtains over the doorway of their cardboard condo. Someone else had set out a geranium plant in front of his packing case. There were even a few families with children in the camp. Several of the youngest played together in a large cardboard box painted with flowers that served as a community playpen.

Smoking a cigarette, Nick was sitting on a broken swivel chair outside a refrigerator case lined with a yellowed mattress. After coming all this way to find him, Ben felt suddenly awkward standing on the doorstep of Nick's pitiful home.

Nick squinted at his presence, as if Ben had stepped into his sunlight. "You get around, don't you, Tex?" he said.

"They told me you were living here."

"Home sweet home." Nick gestured to his cardboard shelter. "I just needs an awning to make it fancy as the Biltmore."

The joke didn't draw a smile from either of them. Ben wondered why he'd ever thought that Nick could help.

"You tracked me down, you must have a reason, boy."

"My momma wants to put us in a foster home," Ben finally blurted out.

Nick leaned back in his broken chair, took a last drag from his cigarette and flipped the butt into the street. "They be worse places."

"Like what?" Ben challenged.

"The missions. The drunk tank."

"They don't put kids in either of those places."

"The street ain't no place to be growing up, either," Nick said, trying to lean back again on the rickety chair.

"I see kids here."

"That don't make it right."

At the very least, Ben had expected more sympathy from him. "Can't you help me?" he asked.

"I be trying to, boy, but you ain't listening too good. Maybe your momma knows better than you. Maybe she wants more for you than growing up on skid row, begging on street corners. . . ."

"How do you know what she wants?" Ben bristled. "You never even met her."

A few tents away a woman in a dirt-streaked dress chased a man away from her barbecue with a frying pan and a string of curses. The people on the street laughed as they watched the fight.

Nick's gaze moved from the fight to take in the entire

campground. "Don't nobody want their kids to live like this," he said softly. "You see my kids down here?"

"You have kids?" Ben had never imagined Nick with children of his own. A father.

"Yeah, I got two boys, one of 'em 'bout your age now."

"Where are they?"

"With their momma, still back in Cleveland I expect . . ." Nick leaned forward, bowed his head.

"You mean you don't even know where they are?"

Nick rose, scowling. "Well they ain't messing 'round down here with drunks and other lowlife, that's for sure. I keep telling you, boy, this ain't no place for you to be. But you don't hear too good, do you? What you keep coming 'round for?"

Ben didn't know what to say.

"Look, there ain't nothing I can do to help you. Now go on, beat it, out of my face." Nick waved his hand at him.

Ben turned and slowly walked away. He had no more ideas of where to look for help.

11

Waiting at the bus stop, Ben tried to find some reason, some logical explanation, anything that could make sense of his family's misery. If there really was a God, surely He wouldn't have brought them here to Los Angeles to live among the poor and homeless without a purpose. Was He testing their faith somehow? Trying to see if they really believed in Him?

Ben's father had no use for the church. "Why should I worry about hell when I'm living it now?" he had shouted at Constance during one bitter fight that Ben had overheard. Had God punished him for his blasphemy? Randall had a Bible and crucifix by his bed and yet he wasn't living any better than Ben's father. What sins had he committed to end up in such poverty?

If he asked his mother the same questions, Ben knew that she would say what she always did when she didn't know how to answer him: "The Lord works in mysterious ways. We can never know the plans He has for us. All we can do is trust in His wisdom."

Ben wasn't sure that even his mother believed that anymore. If she still had faith that the Lord would rescue them, how could she think of breaking up their family?

Ben sat alone on the bus stop bench, watching the grimy pigeons peck at the garbage in the streets, wondering what he would tell Felice and Jube when he returned.

When the bus finally rumbled to a stop beside him, Ben deposited the dollar and a quarter fare in the box and found an empty window seat at the back of the bus. "As long as you do right, right will follow you," his mother and their preacher always said. Ben knew he hadn't been perfect—even this morning he'd stolen—but he'd always tried his best to help his family. Didn't that deserve some mercy and compassion from the Lord? Why weren't his prayers worthy enough to be heard?

Ben closed his eyes and bowed his head in desperation. Though he had no faith that God was listening, he knew nowhere else to turn. Please Lord, he prayed, let my family know what we've done for you to turn your back on us and abandon us to skid row. Help us to understand how we have failed you so that we may change our ways.

Opening his eyes several blocks later, Ben looked out the window and saw his father emerging from a coin laundry on the other side of the street. At least the man appeared to be his father. The man raised his head for a second and stared at the bus, but then a truck passed between them. Ben rose instantly and pulled the cord to signal the driver to stop. The bus had barely come to a halt before Ben shot out the back door and raced across the street. He ran as fast as he could to the other end of the block. But by the time he reached the Laundromat his father had disappeared.

Have I really seen Clyde? Ben wondered. Or have I just imagined him exiting from the Laundromat with his green plastic bag of clothes?

No, it had to be his father, he thought. The man had the same husky build, the same dark, balding hair. He even wore a faded denim jacket exactly like Clyde's. But now, like a desert mirage, he had vanished as magically as he'd appeared.

Ben walked up and down the street several times, checking the open doorways of all the shops he passed. There was no trace of the man he'd seen from the bus.

He returned to the Laundromat. "The man who just left here? Does anybody know him?" he called loudly from the doorway.

A few of the women glanced up at him from their machines, but no one answered. Ben turned to a dark-skinned woman folding her clothes near the entrance. "Did you see which way he went?"

The woman smiled blankly as him. "No speak English," she apologized.

Ben walked outside. Though he hated to give up searching for his father, he was afraid his mother might worry if she found him gone when she returned. It was better to come back another time.

He quickly started for Randall's to break the news to his family. There was no way his mother would put them in foster homes now. The Lord had sent them a sign not to lose hope.

With no money left for bus fare, Ben alternately ran

and walked until, breathless and sweating, he turned down Randall's street. With a start he saw the Chevy parked in front of the cottage. However long his mother had been waiting, though, Ben knew she would forgive him the instant he told her about Clyde.

But it was not his mother sitting at the kitchen table. "This the way you usually take care of your brother and sister?" Randall peered at him through his dark glasses.

"Nosir," Ben said, gasping for breath.

"Yeah, well where the hell've you been?"

Ben glanced at Felice for a sign of how she'd explained his absence. "I told you he went for a walk," she said nervously.

"I'm talking to your brother." Randall rose from the table where he was playing solitaire.

"Where's my mother?" Ben asked.

"Waiting at the welfare office," Randall said. "It could be all afternoon before they get around to seeing her, so she sent me home to check up on you kids. A good thing she did. Now where the hell've you been?"

"No place special," Ben muttered. "Just walking."

Randall limped over to Ben and stood menacingly close. "Didn't your mother teach you to tell the truth?"

Ben nodded, frozen. He didn't know what Randall wanted from him.

"Okay, I'm asking you again, then. Where the hell did you go?"

Ben was afraid that another lie would only make Randall angrier. "Out looking for my father," he said, trying to appear contrite.

The truth seemed to soften Randall a little. "I guess you must miss your daddy," he said.

"Yessir."

"I don't know why, boy. He couldn't wait to get away from you."

Ben stared at Randall's scruffed work boots.

"Well, that's the truth, isn't it? Your daddy ran out on you and your momma and didn't leave a cent behind. That's why you're in the fix you are now. . . ."

"He had his reasons," Ben mumbled. He hated Randall for talking about his father like that.

"Sure he did. He wanted to be free of you."

"You don't know anything about him," Ben said defiantly.

"A Christian man don't run off and leave his family, no matter what troubles he's got."

Ben looked Randall squarely in his dark glasses. Who was he to judge Clyde? "You're trying to make our momma put us in foster homes," he said accusingly.

Randall's face tensed. "Well, maybe you will have to stay with somebody else for a while," he admitted. "But if you want to help your momma get back on her feet, you'll do what she says. If it makes it easier for her to put you in a foster home, then you'd better mind her. Disobeying like you did today only makes it harder for her. You'd think you'd have learned better by now. The last time you ran off, you got all your money stolen. No wonder your momma wanted me to come back and check up on you."

Ben felt his face go hot. Did his mother really not trust him anymore?

"You want to help your mother out, forget about looking for your father," Randall warned, " 'cause even if you found him, your momma don't want him back now."

Ben glanced at his sister to see if she believed Randall. Felice just stood there, hugging Millie.

Let Randall say whatever he wants to, Ben thought. It isn't true.

Bawling Ben out seemed to revive some of Randall's early-morning cheerfulness, though. He heated up a can of tomato soup for lunch and served it to them with stale bread and crackers. Although he tried to make conversation while they ate, Ben, Felice, and Jube had little to say back, and after a while Randall gave it up. When they finished lunch, Ben went into the living room with his brother and sister, turned on the TV set, and waited for Constance to phone from the welfare office for Randall to pick her up.

Randall passed the time at the kitchen table, shuffling his greasy deck of cards, laying them out, one after another, with slow deliberation. Ben remembered his father—after he'd lost his job—sitting the same way at the breakfast table, dull-eyed and unshaven, watching as Constance went off to work and he and Felice set off for school. Sometimes, when Ben returned in the afternoon, his father would still be at the kitchen table, Jube still in his pajamas, and the breakfast and lunch dishes unwashed in the sink. Ben had always dressed Jube, emptied the beer bottles into the trash, and washed the dishes before his mother came home. But none of it had kept his father from leaving.

Yet, once he spoke to his father again, Ben was sure that none of that would matter anymore. Although he was bursting to tell Felice and Jube his news, he didn't want to do it in Randall's presence. There was nothing to do but wait for Constance's call.

Near three o'clock, his mother finally telephoned to say that she was finished. "Now you kids stay put and out of trouble," Randall warned as he left to get her.

As soon as the Chevy pulled away, Ben told the others of his discovery.

Felice and Jube both stared at him as if he'd said he'd seen a ghost.

"It's true," he insisted, recounting the experience in as much detail as he remembered.

Felice listened skeptically. "You weren't very close," she objected. "How can you be sure it was Daddy?"

"Wouldn't you know if you saw him?"

"It's been a long time," she said cautiously. "Maybe he looks different now."

Her wariness surprised him. "Don't you believe me?" he said.

His sister shrugged, unwilling to say one way or the other.

"I believe you, Ben," Jube said without hesitation. "But why did Daddy run away?"

"I told you," Ben explained again. "I was on the bus. He couldn't see me."

"Maybe he did see you," Felice said. "Maybe that's why he ran."

"It is not," Ben said angrily. "Daddy's living somewhere in that neighborhood. If we take Momma's picture of him and show it around, I know someone will recognize him and tell us where he lives. I'm sure of it. . . ."

"Let's see what Momma says," Felice said shortly.

Disgusted, Ben took out his harmonica and went outside to wait for Constance. From time to time he would glance through the torn screen door at his brother and sister. Bored and restless, they had started fighting over the television set, switching channels in the middle of each other's programs. As soon as one of them changed the dial, the other would run up and change it back. It wasn't long before they were both screaming and clawing at each other as they struggled for control of the TV.

Ordinarily Ben would have done something to stop them. But he was too irritated at Felice and too worried about what his mother had done at welfare to bother about their fight.

Finally Ben heard Randall's clunker approaching. The car pulled up in front of the house. Even through the windshield Ben could see how discouraged his mother looked. Randall didn't look very happy, either. He slammed the door of the car and limped ahead of Constance up the walk.

"They're back," Ben called as he stepped inside to alert Felice and Jube. The warning came an instant too late. Jube was standing there with the knob of the channel selector in his hand.

"Now look what you've done!" Felice exclaimed.

Jube thrust the broken knob toward her. "Fix it. Fix it," he said urgently.

Felice grabbed the knob and vainly tried to put it back. "Ben, help us!" Jube pleaded as the sound of Randall's halting step came up the walk.

But there was no time. As Randall opened the door, Felice slipped the knob in her pocket and stood in front of the TV to hide the damage. Jube couldn't hide his fear, though; his anxious face gave them away.

"What's going on?" Randall asked, glaring.

"Nothing," Felice said lightly.

Randall didn't believe her. He came over to see for himself. "Move away from the TV," he ordered.

Felice backed away. "Jube pulled it off by accident," she said. "I was just putting it back. . . ."

"Give it to me!" Randall demanded.

Felice handed it over. "It's broken," he said, and flung it against the wall. She cringed as he grabbed her by the arm. "Didn't I tell you to stay out of trouble?" he yelled, jerking her arm as if he were about to hurl her against the wall as well.

"Stop it!" Constance called from the doorway. She stood there trembling, her face drained of color.

Randall whirled like a cornered animal. "She broke the TV," he snarled, refusing to let go of Felice's arm.

"Let her go. It was just an accident." Constance's voice was low but firm.

"You want her? Take her." Randall shoved Felice toward Constance with so much force that she almost fell.

Ben saw in his mother's face the same mixture of fear and pity with which she used to regard his father when he came home drunk. Randall saw it, too. "Don't give me that preacher's stare," he said with scorn. "Are your kids so precious that you've never hit them before?"

"They're my kids, not yours," she said. "You have no right. . . ."

"You take them, then. If you're such a damn good mother, you feed them and find a place for them to sleep. Because I sure as hell am not going to do it for you." He wheeled around and limped out the door.

Hanging out on skid row, Downtown Los Angeles

Drying sweater near a homeless encampment, Downtown Los Angeles

Tent home on the sidewalk, Downtown Los Angeles

Dusk at the corner of 7th and Spring Streets, Downtown Los Angeles

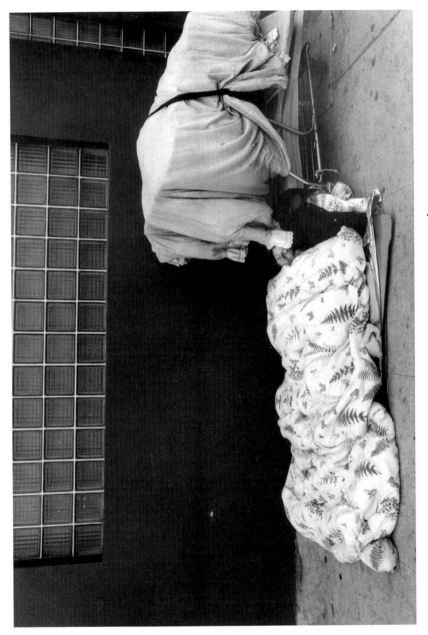

Sleeping woman, Downtown Los Angeles

Early morning in front of the Catholic Worker soup kitchen, Downtown Los Angeles

Homeless person's sign and cart, under the Hollywood Freeway

Kellie, thirty-three-year-old homeless woman, under the Hollywood Freeway

View of Los Angeles looking northwest, from a Downtown building

Albert and Shannon, homeless friends, Downtown Los Angeles

Homeless man resting in the shade, Downtown Los Angeles

Sharon, older homeless woman, Downtown Los Angeles

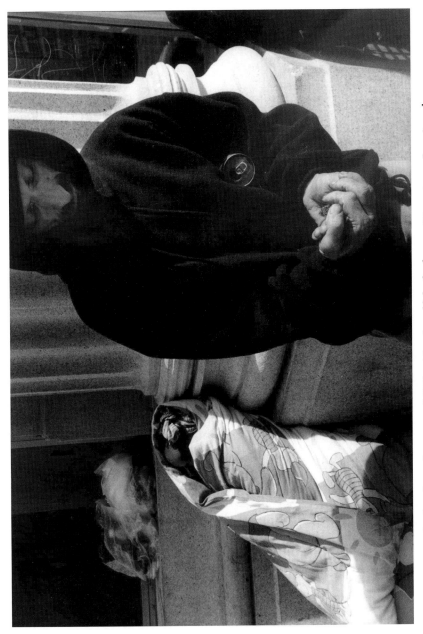

Charles, homeless since 1987, with a handful of tobacco, Downtown Los Angeles

Playing chess on the sidewalk, Downtown Los Angeles

Street scene at 6th and Main Streets, Downtown Los Angeles

Lorraine, homeless twenty-three-year-old mother with her two children, Jessica and Craig, Beverly Hills

Homeless person's belongings, Downtown Los Angeles

Liz, seventeen, and Kyotae, twenty-two, near the Salvation Army drop-in center for homeless young adults, Hollywood

Looking outside from the lobby of the Alexandria Hotel, Downtown Los Angeles

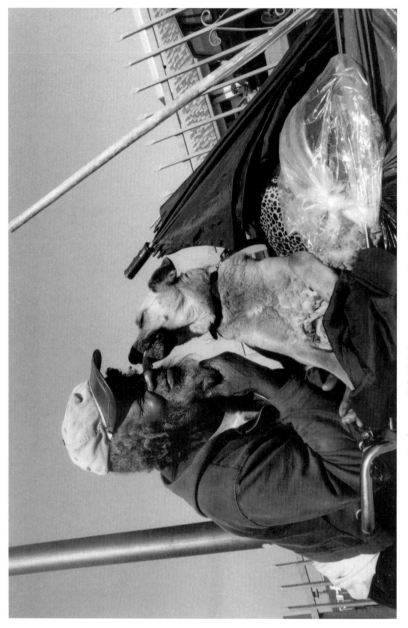

Robert and faithful companion, Daisy, Los Angeles

Jube rushed to cling to his mother's skirt. "He's mean," Jube said, "meaner than Daddy ever was."

"He never liked us," Felice said. "He just pretended to when you were looking."

Outside the Chevy started up and rumbled away.

Constance walked over to the sink, poured a glass of water with a shaking hand.

"You're not going to let him put us in foster homes now, are you?" Ben asked.

She turned to him, stunned. "Where did you get that idea?"

"That's why you went to welfare, isn't it? To set it all up."

"Oh, Ben . . ." she said in a pained voice. "Is that what you thought?"

"We heard you talking to him last night," Felice said accusingly. "You said we'd be better off. . . ."

"No." Constance shook her head. "That's what Randall said. I never believed it."

"But you went to welfare today. . . ."

"Yes, but not to give you children up. I went"—her voice broke—"I went to sign up for welfare. I had to choke down all my pride to do it. But I'd do it again to keep our family together. . . ."

"Why didn't you tell Randall that last night?" he protested.

Constance hung her head, ashamed. "I was afraid . . . of his temper, of what he might do. . . . You saw how angry he got. He was furious when he found out at welfare that they'd only give me money to take care of you children. He didn't know I couldn't get anything if I gave you up."

"How could you even stay with him?" Ben railed.

There were tears in Constance's eyes as she looked at him. "I didn't know where else to go."

"Well, I do," Ben said. "I saw Daddy this morning. I know where to find him."

Constance listened in silence as once more Ben told the story. From the uncertainty in her eyes, though, he wondered if Randall hadn't been right after all about his mother no longer wanting to take Clyde back.

12

Though Ben wanted to begin looking for his father right away, Constance's first concern was with finding a place to spend the night. After Randall's explosion it was clear they couldn't remain there any longer.

The only problem was where to go. With five dollars left they couldn't even afford tickets to an all-night movie theater. A woman at the Heavenly Light Mission had told Constance that sometimes she rode the bus until morning to keep off the streets, but Constance wasn't sure which buses ran all night.

"I'm afraid we've got to go back to that mission," she said as she hurriedly gathered up their belongings.

Felice groaned. "Isn't there anyplace else?"

Ben told them about the shantytown.

"Jube's barely over his cold," Constance objected. "Sleeping outdoors will just make him sick again."

"I'm all better now," Jube said confidently. "No drips." He ran his finger across his nose to show that it was dry.

"It's not just that." Constance looked worried. "I wouldn't feel safe sleeping in the streets."

"It's not the streets," Ben argued. "It's a campground, in the city. They even have portable toilets. . . ."

"I don't like the mission," Jube said. "There's too much crying." Jube has probably shed enough tears there to fill a bathtub himself, Ben thought.

"Why don't you look at the camp?" Ben suggested. "If you don't like it, we can still go to the mission."

Since they had to pass through downtown, anyway, to catch a bus to the general neighborhood of the mission, Constance agreed to stop at the shantytown. Because it was getting late, and they would have to carry their heavy suitcases several blocks, Constance decided it was better to leave them at Randall's until they got settled. In the meantime they stuffed a few clothes and toilet articles into a shopping bag. Felice grabbed Millie, and Jube his firetruck, and they quickly left the house before Randall returned. They were all afraid of what he might do when he got back.

Walking briskly toward the bus stop, Ben felt a renewed sense of hope. So far they had survived all the trials with which God had tested their faith. Surely now He would reward their steadfastness and loyalty by answering their prayers.

"Keep your eyes open," Ben said as they boarded the bus. "We could spot Daddy walking on the street again."

They scanned both sides of the street, all the way downtown, but there was no sign of their father. "I saw him this morning," Ben said. "I really did."

Constance sighed and touched his shoulder. "I know how much you miss him," she said.

"Don't you?" He pulled away from her hand.

She stared out the window at the run-down streets. "We'll come back again and look around here," she said, but Ben didn't hear any conviction in her voice. The escape from Randall's seemed to have drained all her energy.

"Tomorrow morning," Ben insisted.

"As soon as we can." She made no promises. It worried Ben to see how discouraged she'd become. He wondered if Randall's lies had turned her against his father.

They got off the bus a few blocks from Harmony Camp, and Ben led them to the street of shanties. The air was full of smoke and the smell of frying fat as the camp's residents clustered around their cooking fires waiting for their evening meal. The squatters may have been as poor as the people at the mission, but they didn't seem as spiritless to Ben.

His mother was still hesitant. "It's different than I thought," she admitted. "But it's too cold to sleep without blankets—'specially for Jube."

"I know somebody here we can ask," Ben said, guiding them to Nick's cardboard dwelling. Nick was sitting in front of it in his swivel chair, his ski cap pulled to eye level, eating something that looked like chili from a paper plate.

After what he'd told Nick about his mother, Ben felt a little awkward seeing him again. He didn't know what Nick might say.

If Nick was surprised to see him with all his family, he

didn't show it. "You never know who be turning up for dinner," he said, without missing a bite.

Ben noticed his mother gazing uneasily at Nick's scruffy beard and his falling-apart clothes. He introduced them.

"Pleased to meet you," Constance said with effort.

Nick nodded. "Your boy and me, we keep running into each other. I be trying to give him a little advice. . . ."

"We don't have any place to spend the night," Ben interrupted.

Nick gestured to the street with his plastic fork. "Find yourself a spot. The city ain't charging rent yet."

Constance looked uncomfortably at the tents and boxes. "We don't have any blankets or bedrolls," she said.

Nick called over a large woman named Bernice, who wore tight red slacks smudged with dirt and ashes. "These people be friends of mine," he said. "Can you scare 'em up some blankets?"

Bernice waddled over to meet them. "Welcome to Harmony Camp," she said cheerfully. "We ain't got much here, but what we got, we's willing to share."

"Dinner, too?" Jube asked shyly.

"Now, that's a boy after my own heart." She cackled. "First things first." She directed them to the Hari Krishna van around the corner where two orange-robed men with shaved heads were dishing out the chili Nick had been eating. Although there was no meat in it, the food was hot and tasted better than it looked.

When they came back Bernice had found them some fresh blankets that a church group had dropped off at the camp. "This your first time on the street?" she asked.

"We were living in a hotel, but someone stole our money—" Constance began.

"You don't have to explain," Bernice interrupted. "We's all in the same fix. I'm just asking to see how much I got to tell you." She proceeded to help them find a space to sleep and showed them how to make up beds by using newspapers to cover the pavement and the blankets to cover themselves. "It's not supposed to be too cold tonight, so you'll be okay," she said.

Then she took them around and introduced them to the others in the camp. There was a Los Angeles bus driver who had lost his job and had been evicted from his apartment; a waitress from Mobile, Alabama, who had come to L.A. to find a modeling job; and an air-conditioning repairman and his wife from Oklahoma who had driven there looking for more opportunity only to have their car and all their possessions stolen their second day in town.

As night fell, they sat on crates around their small cooking fire talking about the places they'd come from and the hardships they'd been through. The waitress joked that she had been robbed so many times since she'd been living on the streets that she'd placed a card in her change purse saying, "Sorry I can't help out more." The bus driver said he hadn't gotten low enough to steal anything yet, but he wasn't too far from it. When he'd driven his bus, he'd always looked down on the homeless as winos and pillheads who couldn't hold a job. "And there are a few of those around here," he said. But he wasn't a drunk or a doper, and if he could wind up on skid row, anybody could.

Constance listened silently to their stories until the waitress finally asked her how she'd ended up on the streets. Encouraged by their frankness, Constance told them how Clyde had lost his job and come out here, like them, looking for a fresh start and how she'd brought her children out here to find him.

"I know a lot of people are out of work in Texas," the repairman from Oklahoma said. "We tried Houston before we came here."

"Every place we been, people are sleeping in the gutters," his wife said bitterly.

A beam of light suddenly illuminated the camp as a police car drove slowly down the street, directing its spotlight on the sidewalk squatters. A few of the camp's residents waved at the cops, others cursed them. The police car didn't stop. "The only time they come around is when you don't need them," the waitress grumbled.

"I heard talk of their razing this camp," the man from Oklahoma said.

"It don't surprise me," the bus driver said. "We get the businessmen all uptight. They're afraid we might move a few blocks uptown and sleep on their door-steps."

Nick wandered over to their group, holding a bottle in a paper bag. He peered at their faces in the flickering firelight. "Looks like you all just come back from a funeral," he said.

"We were just talking about the cops," the bus driver said.

Nick dismissed them with a tipsy wave of his hand.

"What do cops know? Do they know how to party?" He raised his bottle to his lips and took a long swig. He had obviously been drinking for a while. Ben saw his mother pull Jube closer to her, as if to shield him—or perhaps herself—from Nick's drunkenness.

"What we need's music," Nick said loudly. "Can't party without music." He clapped Ben on the shoulder. "You still got your harmonica, Tex?"

Ben pulled away from his wine-soaked breath. It made him sad and angry to see Nick this way—no different from any other skid-row wino.

"Play us a song, boy, something lively. You know 'Dat Ole Devil Whiskey'?"

Ben shook his head.

"Well, I'm going to sing it for you so you can catch the tune." He began to sing in a rough, wavering voice. "'Dat ole devil whiskey; dat ole devil whiskey; makes me so blue; makes me soooo blue . . .'"

He stopped when he realized Ben hadn't taken out his harmonica. "How come you ain't playing, boy?"

"I don't feel like it," Ben said quietly. The others seemed as embarrassed as he was by Nick's drunken song.

"What's the matter?" Nick needled. "You only play for money?"

"I play when I feel like it," Ben said stiffly.

Constance stood up and took Jube's hand. "I think it's time we got ready for bed," she said.

"Hey, the night be young," Nick said. "The party just be starting."

Constance ignored him. "We need to get settled for the night, Ben," she called.

"In a minute," he said. There was something he wanted to find out.

"Don't be long," she cautioned.

The couple from Oklahoma got up as well.

"My singing chasing you away, too?" Nick said.

They laughed uncomfortably and said they were just going to stretch their legs. The bus driver and waitress asked if they could join them on their walk.

"Sure," the Oklahoma man said. "Four's safer than two at night."

That left Nick and Ben alone by the dying fire. Nick pulled up a vacant crate and seated himself unsteadily. Ben had never seen him this shaky before. "Your momma don't think much of me," he said. "Reminds me of my wife." His dry laugh turned into a cough and he took another pull from his bottle to stop it.

"Let me have a taste." Ben reached for the bottle.

For the first time Nick actually seemed surprised. "You got enough troubles, boy, without adding this."

"Just a taste," Ben said. "What harm's that going to do?"

Nick shrugged, as if it were hopeless to explain, wiped the mouth of the bottle, and passed it over to him.

Ben took a gulp of the sour liquid and spit it out. "Why do you drink this stuff?" He finally spoke the question he'd never had the courage to ask his father.

"To get well, boy. To get well." Nick took the bottle back and raised it to his mouth again. "This be my medicine. My medicine for hard times."

"But it only makes you sick," Ben said bitterly, thinking of all the drunks he'd seen passed out on the sidewalk.

"If I stop drinking, I be even sicker, boy."

"How do you know? Have you even tried?"

Nick's face contorted with anger. "Who you be to be telling me how to lead my life?" He drained the last of the wine, staggered to his feet, and flung the bottle into the street where it shattered.

"You worry about yourself, boy. You the one who don't know how to get along down here." He took a step forward and fell to the ground.

Ben went to help him up and saw that he'd passed out. He went over to Nick's packing crate, picked up one of his foul-smelling blankets, and covered him with it for the night.

13

Waking before dawn the next morning, Ben lay on his back on the pavement, gazing at the mud-colored sky, and tried to imagine himself at the campgrounds in Oklahoma. His face was wet with dew as it had been each morning by the river and there was the comforting spit and crackle of kindling as someone began a fire. If he pretended the distant hum of traffic was the water lapping against the bridge, and if he kept his eyes fixed on the sky and didn't let them wander to the crumbling brick building across the street, he could almost transport himself back to the Mountain Fork with his father. Then the wind shifted and, instead of wood smoke drifting over him, he inhaled the sickening fumes of the garbage-clogged streets. Turning to avoid the stink, he found himself face to face with a smelly old man he'd never seen before, sleeping a foot away under a blanket of dirty newspapers, like an animal burrowed under a pile of trash.

Ben sprang to his feet, with the shock of someone

waking from a nightmare. His whole body ached from sleeping on the pavement and, with the cold and the fright the old man had given him, he could not stop his shivering.

Constance was already up, warming her hands over the small fire that Bernice had built in her gas-can stove. Seeing Ben awake, Constance put an arm around him and led him over to the fire. With Jube and Felice still asleep, he could huddle quietly in her warmth, the way he used to when he was still a child.

At the campsite in Oklahoma, his father always had a pot of coffee on the fire when Ben woke in the morning. There was no coffee brewing this morning, no eggs or bacon waiting to be fried. For some, like Nick, perhaps not even food would have stirred them from their drunken sleep. Someone had dragged Nick back to his mattress last night, where he lay curled up like a bear hibernating for the winter. Maybe, Ben thought, that is one of the reasons street people drink so much. The longer the wine knocks you out, the less time you have to worry about how to get through the day.

Although it was only a little past dawn, several of the squatters emerged from their dwellings and straggled over to the fire. Still unwashed, their faces creased with sleep or lack of it, they stood around smoking a cigarette butt or rubbing their hands together against the chill morning wind.

Observing the glowering sky, several people predicted rain. "I thought California was the land of sunshine," the man from Oklahoma said. "Not in February," Bernice said. "A little rain's not bad," another man observed. "Clears the air and the garbage from the streets." The bus driver shook his head. "It'll take more than a good rainstorm to clean these streets."

Felice and Jube woke up within a few minutes of each other and joined the group around the fire. Jube's nose was running again and Constance draped a blanket around his shoulders. Felice's face was raw and blotchy, and Ben guessed she hadn't slept anymore than he. The cold and the impossibility of finding a comfortable position on the pavement and the police cars periodically sweeping the streets with their searchlights had kept him up much of the night.

"The mission was better," Felice said, glaring at Ben as if last night was all his fault.

"You didn't want to go there, either," he reminded her.

"Hush, both of you!" Constance quickly cut them off.

"When you don't have money, there ain't no good place to go, sugar," Bernice spoke to Felice. "We all be stuck between a rock and a hard place."

"A wet place, it looks like," the bus driver said, glancing at the sky.

Since the Gibsons had no raincoats to protect themselves against the coming storm, Bernice told Constance where to look for plastic covering. They left their shopping bag of clothes with her and set out to find the plastic quickly so they could be back in time to line up with the others in the camp for a free meal at the Catholic Worker's soup kitchen.

The warehouses where Bernice directed them were just a few blocks away. Two other men were already digging through the dumpsters when they arrived. Ben remembered how repelled he'd been to see Nick foraging through the garbage. Now, less than two weeks later, they were doing the same thing.

"What are we going to do now?" Felice asked when they had found enough plastic wrapping to fashion crude raincoats.

"Well, we're going to go back and get some food and then go out to the mission," Constance said. "We can't sleep outside tonight, not in the rain."

"I don't want to sleep in the mission," Jube said. "I want to sleep in a bed, in a house, like we used to."

"Well, you can't," Felice said sternly, "because houses are for rich people, and we're very poor."

"Why?" Jube asked. "Why are we poor?"

"'Cause Daddy ran out on us," Felice said matter-of-factly.

"If we go back to the Laundromat now maybe we can find him," Ben urged, desperately trying to revive their hopes. Had they all given up on his father except him?

Constance looked up at the darkening sky. "We'd better start for the mission. I don't want to get caught in the rain."

"No," Ben refused. If they went back to the mission now, he knew it would be a long time before they could look for his father again. With no money, and no prospects, they might be trapped at the church for months.

"Your brother's getting sick again," Constance said. "He can't be out in the rain."

"Then you take him to the mission," Ben said. "I'm going to look for Daddy myself." He started to walk away.

"Wait! Ben!" she called after him.

He turned around.

She looked up at the sky again. "Maybe we can make it before the storm," she yielded. "But when I say it's time to stop, you've got to come with us."

Ben readily agreed.

Clutching their flimsy wrappers to their sides, they hurried down the cracked and crumbling sidewalks. The wind whipped and tugged at the plastic, lifting it like giant sails which speeded them along.

When they reached the Laundromat, they found only a few people washing their clothes. None of them recognized Clyde's picture. Felice looked at Ben and rolled her eyes. Ben ignored her and quickly led them to the shoe repair shop next door.

The shoemaker couldn't help either, though, nor could the Korean grocer at the corner. They tried one store after another, all with the same results. A few people thought Clyde's picture looked familiar, but no one knew his name or where to find him.

"My feet hurt," Jube complained after they had tried about a dozen stores.

Constance picked Jube up to soothe him and glanced at the sky, which was growing more and more threatening. "I think we'd better be starting back," she said.

"Just a few more places," Ben pleaded.

"One more place," Constance said firmly. "That's all."

Ben scanned the remaining shops on the street and picked the printer's. The owner was busy inking a press when they entered. He wiped his hands on his black apron and studied the photograph Constance handed him. He didn't recognize Clyde, either.

Ben felt faint as he watched the printer hand the photo back to his mother. There was nothing more he could do to save his family. They were now as lost, as homeless, as any other family on the street.

"Wait!" the printer called as they started to leave. "Is that the only picture you have of him?"

Constance told him that it was.

He peered at them over the counter with their dirty clothes and cast-off plastic rain gear. His sympathetic gaze made Ben suddenly conscious of how down-and-out they must look.

"What you need," the printer said, "is a handbill to leave with people in case they run across your husband."

"I can't afford anything like that," Constance said uncomfortably.

With unexpected kindness—as surprising to Ben as the kindness of the people who'd given him money in the street—the printer offered to make one up for free.

"I can't ask you to do something like that," Constance said.

"No trouble," he replied. "I'll just make a copy of the photograph and put down a number where they can contact you."

Ben saw the color rising in his mother's cheeks. "We're kind of in between places right now," she mumbled. "We don't have a phone."

"Well, why don't we just put my number down, then," the printer said, "and you can check back here to see if anyone has called."

"I'm much obliged," Constance said, staring at her worn shoes.

It took only a few minutes for the printer to copy a hundred handbills on his machine. Underneath the photograph he'd listed his number. Below that it said, "Anyone with information regarding this man, please call."

Touched by the printer's generosity, Constance thanked him once again.

"I hope it works," he said.

He has at least given us another chance, Ben thought.

Thunder rumbled in the distance as they left the shop, reminding Felice that she had left her doll with their belongings. They hurried back toward Harmony Camp to try to pick up the doll and their shopping bag before the storm broke. Ben lagged behind his family, passing out handbills to shop owners, or hanging them on telephone poles, like posters of lost dogs. He wondered what his father would think if he found one.

They were still several blocks away from the camp-grounds when the rain began to fall. They threw the plastic sheets over their heads and dashed down the block to an abandoned movie theater whose marquee provided some protection from the downpour.

"I shouldn't have left Millie," Felice said as they watched the rain lash the streets. "She could drown, or wash away." For the first time since they arrived in Los Angeles, she began to cry. Burying her face against Constance's breast, she wept as steadily as the rain.

Constance held her daughter and softly stroked her hair. "It's going to be all right, honey," she said. "It's going to be all right."

After all the terrible things that had happened to them, all the disappointments and hardships they had suffered, it unsettled Ben to see Felice fall apart now, over her silly doll. Jube was just as stunned to see his sister crying and hung on to Ben as if he were all that kept him from being washed into the watery streets. Even when Ben put his arm around him and held him close, Jube could not stop his shivering.

They huddled together by the boarded-up theater for a long time, waiting for the rain to subside. "I know all this is for some reason," Constance said as she watched the cars splash by them. "I'm sure one day we'll understand God's purpose in this."

It made Ben furious to hear her speak that way. "God doesn't even know we're here," he said bitterly.

"Sometimes it may seem like that," Constance said gently, "but I know the Lord cares about us and that He won't make us suffer any more than we can bear."

Ben felt something strengthen in her even as she said it. He wished that he could believe as much as she did. But what good had all her faith brought them?

After about a half hour the rain finally began to slacken. "Let's hurry before it starts up again," Constance said.

"Where?" Ben asked.

She pointed up the street to the spire of a church rising above the other buildings.

Ben carried his brother to protect him from the puddles on the rain-drenched streets. By the time they reached the cathedral, though, his own tennis shoes and socks were soaked through to the skin.

To his surprise Ben discovered the old stone church was Catholic, but whatever the religion, it was at least a place to keep warm and dry. Although he expected the building to be packed with other street people taking refuge from the rain, only about a dozen people were sitting or kneeling when they arrived. And most of them looked like regular churchgoers. Constance led them to an empty row of seats toward the back of the darkened church, where they sat dripping on the polished wooden pews.

With its white columns and vaulted ceiling, the church was more like the Biltmore Hotel than the Heavenly Light Mission. There were silver candlesticks on the marble altar, a tall gold crucifix, and large stained-glass windows. Wet and muddy, Ben felt as out of place there as he had in the Biltmore.

While Constance knelt and prayed he studied the pictures of Christ on the windows. There were scenes of Jesus playing with children, teaching his disciples, even tending a flock of sheep, but none that showed him with the poor and the outcast. Maybe that was why most of the men and women in the church didn't look as if they lived on the streets.

Gradually a few more people entered the church. Ben watched them cross themselves, kneel, and pray, believing, like his mother, that somehow God listened to each one of them. At this very moment, all over the world, perhaps millions of people are praying for God to take notice of them, Ben thought. How can we expect God to hear our prayers above all the rest?

At noon the church bells rang, more lights came on, and Ben realized that the people had gathered there for a service. Two robed priests entered from the door beside the altar, and the congregation rose. Constance stood up with them, but Ben remained in his seat. Felice and Jube didn't pray, either. Jube lay with his head on Felice's lap and slept while she sat with folded arms glaring at the altar.

From his mother's hesitancy, Ben didn't think she had ever been to a Catholic mass before or knew what to do. Although the service was different from the Baptist church at home, the message was the same. "Turn to the Lord in your need, and you will live," the congregation recited. "Happy are they who hope in the Lord." Constance followed the actions of the other worshippers, rising and kneeling when they did, repeating their responses to the prayers. Ben remained in his seat, damp and stiff and full of anger. His mother kept glancing at him each time she rose or knelt, hoping, perhaps, that he might change his mind. Ben didn't care. Watching her lose herself in the service, eyes closed, lips moving fervently, he wondered if she was praying for him as well.

After a number of prayers and readings from the Bible, two ushers began moving up and down the aisles with the collection basket. Since his family was sitting so far in the back and were obviously street people, Ben hoped they would ignore them. The thought didn't even appear to cross the mind of the usher heading toward them. Or his mother's, either. It startled Ben to see her reach for her wallet and place one of their last dollars in the collection basket. Felice looked at her as if she couldn't believe what she'd just seen, either. Was Constance giving away their bus fare to the mission? How could this rich church possibly need the money more than their family? Did his mother believe that her offering would make God look more favorably on her prayers?

Constance saw their disapproval. " 'And though I have all faith, so that I could remove mountains, and have not charity, I am nothing,' " she quoted Scripture under her breath.

Near the close of the service the worshippers went up to the altar to receive communion from the priests. Since his mother was not a Catholic, Ben understood why she remained in her seat. Even so, he couldn't help thinking that no matter where his family went, they never seemed to be among the blessed.

When the mass was finished, everyone stood up as the priests exited from the church. The rain had started up again and people stopped at the cathedral doors to put on their raincoats and open their umbrellas before they ventured out into the storm. Ben looked at Constance to see what she was going to do. "Let's just keep praying," she said. She knelt and clasped her hands together.

Within a few minutes they were the only people left in the church. The janitor turned off the lights on the altar, closed and locked one of the doors. Ben suddenly realized why no other street people took shelter here. The church was only open during services.

Row by row the janitor noisily went through the seats, putting the missals back in their racks, inspecting for forgotten clothing. When he came to their row, he didn't say anything, but his impatient glance clearly indicated that it was time for them to leave.

Constance continued praying.

The custodian turned out all the lights except for the two front chandeliers. Then he snuffed out the candles in the silver candlesticks. Standing on the altar, he looked back at them uncertainly, as if trying to decide whether to tell them to leave. Finally, he disappeared through the door behind the altar.

A few moments later he reappeared with the younger of the two priests who had conducted mass. The man had taken off his robe and was now dressed in his regular black suit and white collar. He came down the aisle and stopped in front of Constance. In a glance he took their situation in.

"The church is closing now," he said kindly. "Is there anything I can help you with?"

Constance looked up and met his eyes. "We have no food, no money, no place to live. . . ."

Like the printer earlier, the priest did not turn away. "I'm glad you came here," he said.

14

The Gibsons waited in the vestry, drinking juice and eating cookies, while Father Beaudry closed the door of his office and tried to see what he could do for them. An hour passed on the vestry clock, and then a second one. The closed door made it difficult to make out what the priest was saying on the phone, but Ben could hear the frustration mounting in his voice. Ben wasn't surprised that the priest couldn't find anyone to take them in.

After almost two and a half hours, Father Beaudry finally opened the door of his office. With a tired smile, he told them he had found space for their family at the Salvation Army shelter.

"I called that shelter several times and they never had room," Constance said, amazed.

"Well, God must have heard your prayers today," the priest said, "for an hour ago another family moved out."

Constance's eyes filled with tears as she clasped the priest's hand and thanked him for his help. Ben didn't know how she could be so grateful for a place she hadn't even seen. The last time she thought that God had answered her prayers, they had ended up at the Heavenly Light Mission.

The janitor drove them to the shelter. Although the storm had slowed to a drizzle, the streets were still slick with rain. Streams of garbage flowed along the curbs into the sewers. Ben wondered if any of the posters of his father were still hanging on the telephone poles.

"Can we stop for Millie?" Felice asked.

"We'll go back for her tomorrow," Constance said.

"It'll be too late then," Felice said. "Millie will be ruined."

"I'm sure Bernice'll keep her safe and dry," Constance said. "But right now we need to get to the Salvation Army. I don't want to lose our place."

"What's a 'Salvation Army'?" Jube asked.

"A place for people whose mothers can't take care of them," Felice said, glowering.

Constance didn't answer. She looked out into the streets where people still huddled in doorways from the rain. Ben couldn't tell what she was thinking anymore, about Millie, his father, anything. He clutched the remaining handbills in his jacket. *No matter what she decides,* Ben vowed, *I will not give up looking for my father.*

The church janitor let them off in front of a small, three-story, cement building, a few blocks away from the high-rent district where Nick had taken Ben to play his harmonica. Walking past it on the street, Ben wouldn't have suspected anybody lived there.

There was a small waiting room at the entrance. Constance told the lady at the reception desk who they were, and a few minutes later a frizzy-haired black woman walked into the lobby and greeted them. She wore blue jeans and large round glasses that had a slight rose-colored tint. "Hi, I'm Lorraine." She shook all their hands in a firm, energetic grip. "You look like you've had a rough day. C'mon, I'll show you around and get you some coffee."

She took them upstairs in the elevator. On the first floor were offices, she explained, on the second and third floors, the rooms where the residents lived. They got out on the third floor and Lorraine led them down the rust-carpeted hallway. The building could have been any modern hotel or apartment complex. There were even small video cameras mounted on the walls. Ben wondered if the cameras were to guard against intruders or to watch the residents of the shelter.

Lorraine unlocked the door to their room. It was small and plain, with two sets of bunk beds, a dresser, and a separate bathroom with tub and shower. The beds had been freshly made with clean sheets and the bathroom smelled as if it had just been scrubbed. There was even a picture of a waterfall hanging crookedly on the wall. Lorraine straightened the picture. "Well, this is it," she said. The Gibsons looked around in amazement.

"This room is just for us?" Felice said.

Lorraine smiled. "It's why they call us the Biltmore of shelters. Let me give you the rest of the tour and you can settle in here later."

With nothing but the clothes on their backs, they didn't have much settling to do. "We have some suitcases," Constance said self-consciously, "but we had to leave them at this place where we were staying. . . ."

"Oh, you don't need to worry about that now," Lorraine said. "We have a box you can look through for some fresh clothes."

"We did get a little dirty in the storm," Constance said gratefully.

"That's what we have a laundry for," Lorraine said. "C'mon, I'll show you." She led them to the laundry room at the end of the hall and then down to the second floor to see the rest of the shelter. There was a small playroom with books and toys, a rooftop deck with picnic tables and some large plastic blocks for climbing, a lounge with a TV set that Lorraine said couldn't go on until six in the evening, and a dining room where she took them for milk and coffee.

They sat at a table with their drinks and she explained the shelter's principle rules. Residents had to sign in and out each time they entered or left the building. Curfew was ten o'clock. If anyone tried to come in later, they wouldn't be readmitted. There was a routine check every night between ten and eleven to make sure everyone was in their rooms. School-age children—Ben and Felice—had to attend the local elementary or junior high schools while they lived at the shelter. Children under six—Jube—had to be with their mothers at all times. And no drugs or alcohol. Period. If any were discovered, the family would be immediately evicted. "I'll give you a booklet where it's all written down," Lorraine said.

"If we follow those rules, how long can we stay?" Constance said hesitantly.

Lorraine put down her coffee cup. "Right now our

limit's two months. It used to be two weeks, if you can imagine that. Two weeks isn't much time to find afford-able housing in this city. But in two months it can be done. We'll work with you to make it happen. That's our goal here—to help families find permanent hous-ing. We're a small shelter, just fifty-four beds, enough to take only twelve to fifteen families at a time, but we do as much as we can to get you back on your feet. We'll start tomorrow morning."

"What happens if . . . if we can't find anyplace?" Constance said, staring at her coffee cup.

"There's a long time before we have to worry about that," Lorraine said.

Constance turned her head away.

"Is something wrong?" Lorraine asked.

Constance covered her eyes, trying to fight back her tears. "We've been on the streets, in those hotels"— her voice broke—"nobody should have to live that way. . . ."

Lorraine reached over and took Constance's hand. "You're right," she said sympathetically. "Nobody should."

The tears rolled down Constance's cheeks. "I didn't think anyone would believe we started out with good intentions and ended up like this."

"That's why we're here," Lorraine said, still holding tightly to Constance's hand. "There are two, maybe three million homeless in this country. Nobody knows how many, really. We just know the number's growing every day, and that more and more are families like yours."

"I thought it was all my fault," Constance sobbed. "That I wasn't the right kind of mother, that I let my kids down. Most mothers don't have kids in shelters. . . ."

Felice reached over and put an arm around Constance. Ben wondered if his sister was sorry for her angry words in the car. "Don't cry, Momma," she said. "This is a good place to stay."

"I know it's hard to see that right now," Lorraine said, "but I hope in time you'll agree with your daughter."

Felice and Jube both tried to brush away their mother's tears. "You said God would not give us more than we could bear," Felice said softly.

Still Constance kept on crying.

Lorraine rose and patted her on the shoulder. "Why don't I take your children and introduce them to some of the other kids here?"

Jube and Felice eagerly followed her, but Ben remained at the table.

Constance dried her eyes with a napkin. "She's very nice," she said as she watched Lorraine leave the dining room.

Ben hadn't made up his mind yet. He was waiting to see if Lorraine would help them find Clyde. "Are you going to call the printer?" he asked.

She looked as if she'd forgotten all about it. "I will," she said. "I just need a few more minutes."

Ben waited with her in the dining room while she finished her coffee and composed herself, then followed her to the staff office, whose windows looked out into the lounge. On the desk inside was a television monitor which displayed the pictures from the cameras mounted in the hallways.

Ben watched through the office window as Constance made the call. He didn't need to hear her conversation to tell that there was no news of his father.

"No one called," Constance said when she came out, "but I told him where we're staying now in case anybody does."

"We still got posters we can put up," Ben said. "As soon as the rain stops."

Constance put her hand on his shoulder. "Posters aren't going to do much good if your father isn't planning to come back."

After they had bathed and put on fresh clothes that they had selected from the box of used goods donated to the shelter, they went into the dining room for dinner. Seated at one of the tables was the black youth from the Athens. The boy's surprise quickly turned into a sneer. "I thought you were moving to Bel-Air," he said.

Ben's face reddened. "What are you doing here?" he asked.

"What d'you think?" the boy said.

"You know each other?" The boy's mother addressed Ben. She was a thin, hollowed-eyed woman with close-cropped hair who did not look very well.

Constance answered for him. "We stayed at the Athens. . . ."

"Oh, that rattrap . . ." the woman said in disgust. "Somebody should burn it down."

She invited them to pull up chairs and eat with her and her son. The Gibsons got their food from the kitchen—short ribs, mashed potatoes, and beans—and sat down at the table with the woman and her son, who introduced themselves as Helen and Larry. Helen was much friendlier than Larry. Within a few minutes she was telling them her story. Two months earlier she had walked out on her husband in New York and come to

L.A. with Larry because she'd heard it was easier to find a job in California. One misfortune had quickly led to another, though, and like the Gibsons, she and her son had ended up first at the Athens, and now at the Salvation Army shelter, which they'd been waiting to get into for weeks until a place had finally opened up the day before.

Larry fiddled with the bones on his plate, shifted in his chair, and stared out the window as if he were bored by everything that had happened to them in the past two months. No matter how much he pretended not to care, Ben knew now it was all a lie.

"So what about you? How did you get here?" Helen asked Constance. Ben concentrated on his food while his mother briefly recounted all their troubles.

"I know it's none of my business," Helen said when Constance had finished, "but why are you still chasing after your husband? He'll only drag you down with him."

"I've been praying every night that he's changed," Constance said.

Helen looked doubtful. "You can pray all you want for him, but God helps those who help themselves. Unless you get up off your assets and do something for yourself, nothing's going to change."

Constance stiffened at her rebuke.

"Listen, honey," Helen said with feeling. "After you've been bounced around awhile in this pinball machine, either you toughen up or else you break into little pieces. If prayer was enough to make things right, nobody'd be poor."

Ben waited for his mother to defend herself. Constance was silent.

145

Helen rose from the table. "Good meeting you," she said.

Larry got up with her. "I guess I'll be seeing you around," he muttered.

Ben didn't see any way to avoid it, either.

The next morning, after breakfast, Constance met alone with Lorraine in a downstairs office to discuss the Gibsons' problems. Ben and Felice waited in the lounge with Jube, working on a picture puzzle for over an hour, until Lorraine finally called upstairs and invited them to join their mother.

Constance and Lorraine were sitting at a table drinking coffee like old friends when Ben entered the room. "Your mom and I've been having a very good talk," Lorraine said, pulling out a chair next to her for Felice. Jube hopped onto Constance's lap while Ben took a seat at the far end of the table.

"Your mom has been telling me all about your family," Lorraine went on. "But I wanted to hear from you children, too."

"About what?" Ben said suspiciously. He wondered just what his mother had told Lorraine.

"Well, a lot of things have happened to your family this year, and I'd like to know how you feel about them. . . ."

Ben didn't say anything. How did she expect them to feel about being poor and homeless?

Felice looked over at her mother. Constance nodded encouragingly.

"Are you going to find us a place to live?" Felice asked.

"That's one of the things we try to do here," Lorraine said, "help people to find a decent place to live. But before we can start doing that, there are a lot of important decisions your family's going to have to make. And the first one is whether you want to return to El Paso. . . ."

"Why should we go back there?" Ben interrupted. "We came here to find our daddy."

Lorraine turned to him. "And what if he isn't here in L.A.?"

"I saw him on the street, two days ago. Didn't Momma tell you?" He looked at Constance accusingly.

"Yes, she did say that," Lorraine said. "But why don't you tell me about it."

"I was on the bus and he was across the street, coming out of a laundry. . . ."

"Did he see you?"

Ben remembered the instant Clyde raised his head and stared in his direction. Was it possible that his father had recognized him? "He was too far away," he said.

"Your dad's been gone five months now," Lorraine said. "That's a long time. What makes you think he wants to come back?"

Ben couldn't believe that she would even ask. "He's our daddy," he said indignantly.

"And do you feel the same way, Felice?" Lorraine turned to her.

Felice looked at the table and slowly shook her head. "He didn't even say good-bye," she said.

"He came here to make a fresh start," Ben protested. "It's easier on his own."

"What if he wants to continue that way?" Lorraine asked.

"You don't know that," Ben said angrily.

Constance turned to him. "She's right, Ben. We've got to think about it."

Ben wouldn't look at her.

"I think it's something you all need to consider when you start planning for the future," Lorraine said. She turned to Constance. "The most important thing you have to decide is if you still want to stay in Los Angeles, even without your husband."

"I'm afraid there's not much to go back to in Texas," Constance said. "We sold most of what we had to come to L.A."

"I realize that, but it's still a big decision to relocate here."

"I know. I'd need to find work, a place to live. . . ." Constance faltered at the difficulties of accomplishing either.

"It may be hard, but it's not impossible," Lorraine said confidently. "You're a strong woman, Constance, stronger than I think you realize. In the last year and a half you've had to be both mother *and* father to your children, yet you've managed to keep your family together. There's no reason why you can't continue." She picked up her clipboard and glanced at the notes she had written. "When I look down this list at the jobs you've worked and the skills you have, I see a very capable woman. With lots of marketable skills."

A blush the color of Lorraine's glasses spread slowly across Constance's cheeks.

"These are important decisions, though, for the whole family, and I know you'll want to think about them carefully. Talk it over together and we'll discuss it in a few days. Whatever you decide, we'll try to help you make it work."

"What about helping us find our father?" Ben said.

Lorraine fixed her full attention on him. "I'm afraid there's not much I can do about that," she replied. "Have you spoken to the police?"

"Why?" Ben said in alarm.

"Because the police are the ones responsible for missing persons."

"He's not missing," Ben insisted. "I told you. I saw him walking on the street."

"*Away*, Ben. You saw him walking *away*," Constance said.

Ben rose abruptly and fled the office.

15

The rain kept up intermittently throughout the week-
end. Felice stood at the bedroom window, watching
the cars splash through the gray wet streets, worrying
about Millie. Because of the weather and the distance
Constance hadn't been willing to go back for her yet.

"It's too late now. I know it," Felice said to Ben.
"Even if we find her, she'll be ruined."

"She's plastic," Ben said. "The rain won't hurt her.
It'll just give her a good bath."

But Felice felt so bad about leaving Millie behind
that nothing could convince her that her doll would survive. "Millie's so sad," she said, her eyes filling with
tears. "She thinks I'm never coming back for her."

They had no home, no money, no future, and all
Felice could think about was a dumb plastic doll.
"C'mon, stop crying," he said. "If Momma won't go
back for her, I will."

"Really?" She dabbed at her eyes.

"Really."

"When? When will you get her?"

"Monday, when we have to go to school. But don't tell anyone."

"Why not, Ben?"

"Just don't tell anyone. Okay?" He didn't want his mother knowing he was planning to ditch his first day of school. But just because she'd given up on his father didn't mean he was going to. He thought of the father and son they had met at the Heavenly Light Mission. "I don't know what I would've done without him," he remembered the father saying. One day both his mother and father would say the same of him.

Monday morning after breakfast all the school-aged children in the shelter set off for school. Felice joined the four other children who were already attending elementary school and Ben left the shelter with Larry, who had begun classes at junior high school the week before.

As soon as they reached the bus stop, Ben told him that he had other plans.

Larry's expression indicated Ben was making a big mistake. "You think they won't check up on you?"

"What if they do?" Ben tried to sound braver than he felt.

"They'll kick you out, man." Larry snapped his fingers. "Just like that. Good-bye shelter, hello street."

Ben considered the risk. Without his father, he didn't care much where they lived. "I got to do it," he said.

"Well, I'm sure not lying for you," Larry said with sudden vehemence. "If Lorraine asks, I'll tell her." He sounded like he hoped she would.

Ben shrugged. Larry's meanness didn't frighten him anymore. He could see that it was just his way of trying to hide his own fear.

Ben left him at the bus stop and headed downtown on foot to Harmony Camp, posting a few of the handbills of his father as he went. He planned to go out to the Laundromat and search that area again, but he wanted to pick up Felice's doll first. Maybe Nick or someone else at the camp would even have some ideas about where to look for his father. Ben realized that he'd never shown Nick Clyde's picture. It was possible that Nick might recognize him and lead Ben right to him. If Nick wasn't drunk, of course, or passed out somewhere in an alley.

As Ben neared the shantytown, several police cars and city trucks passed him, heading in the same direction. Seeing them turn the corner to the campgrounds, Ben ran to find out what was happening. He raced around the corner to see the street clogged with police cars and maintenance trucks.

Cops with drawn billy clubs were trying to clear the sidewalks of people so that the maintenance men could tear down their shanties. The residents of the camp scrambled frantically to gather up their possessions as the men in hard hats and face masks threw their bedding and furniture into the street.

"No-no-no-no!" an old man cried helplessly as he struggled to save his bedroll.

A cop yanked another bedraggled down-and-outer from his cardboard packing case. The man staggered to his feet, dazed and bewildered.

Others swore angrily at the cops. Television cameras recorded it all for the evening news.

Ben searched for Nick but didn't see him. Then he spotted Bernice and two other women surrounding a female cop who didn't look very happy to be there. "*Why? Why* are you doing this?" Bernice screamed at her, inches from her face.

The police officer tried to stay calm. "Orders of the mayor. It's illegal to sleep on the streets."

"*Where?* Where are we going to go?" another woman yelled at her.

The cop shook her head. "You'll sleep in jail if you don't clear out."

The three women stood their ground. "What are you going to arrest us for?" Bernice shouted. "For being homeless? Is that a crime?"

The cop finally lost her patience, raised her billy club, and started to shove Bernice toward a patrol car.

Ben rushed toward Bernice's plastic lean-to to find Millie before the garbagemen got to her. A cop grabbed him by the shoulder and held him back.

"My sister's doll . . ." Ben pleaded.

It made no difference to the cop. "Clear out, kid," he ordered.

A bulldozer rolled down the sidewalk, crumpling the makeshift shelters like used paper plates. The men in hard hats followed with shovels and brooms, sweeping up everything in their path. Broken chairs and crates, torn bedclothes and mattresses, a geranium plant.

When the bulldozer reached Bernice's jumble of wood and plastic, Ben turned away, unable to watch.

On the other side of the street a woman in a black dress and high heels put on garden gloves and started sweeping the sidewalk as she spoke to a television crew. "We can't have people living in unsanitary condi-

tions like this. It's a danger to public health and safety."
She wrinkled her nose as she swept some garbage into
the gutter. "This whole area has to be hosed down now
and disinfected."

Ben felt a rough hand on his shoulder. "This ain't no
time to be gawking, boy."

Ben turned to find Nick standing behind him with his
overloaded shopping cart. "C'mon, time to split," he
said, steering Ben firmly toward the corner. "You want
to watch this mess, you can catch it later on the five
o'clock news."

When they reached the corner, Ben stopped to look
back. The bulldozer had ripped through most of the
shanties, and the hard hats were finishing off the rest
with shovels. They were loading the portable toilets
onto a pickup truck and unwinding long firehoses from
one of the trucks. In half an hour there would be no
trace of the camp.

"They have no right to do that," Ben said bitterly.

"They not asking you, boy," Nick answered. His gaze
lingered a moment on what was left of the camp-
grounds. Then he turned away, as if there were no
point in wasting any more energy on rubble.

"Where's your momma, Tex?" he asked, suddenly
remembering her.

"Back at the shelter."

Nick looked confused. "What shelter?"

"The Salvation Army."

"When'd you go there?"

Ben realized that Nick had no idea that his family had
even left the camp. "We left Thursday," he said. "Didn't
you notice?"

Nick straightened the ski cap on his head. "I don't keep track of nobody else's business, boy. I got my own problems to worry about." His stubbled face was pale and sweaty.

"You run home to your momma now and tell her she got out just in time," he said. He shoved his cart and started off.

"Wait. Where you going?" Ben followed him.

"To get myself a short dog."

Ben looked at him blankly.

"A bottle of T-bird. Wine." Nick glared at him with bleary eyes.

Ben guessed he'd been drinking ever since they'd left. "Are you okay?" he said, worried.

"No, I ain't. I need a drink to get me well." As they walked, Nick pulled out the coins in his pocket and counted them. "Damn!" he said. "I'm short. You lend me forty cents?"

Ben felt the anger clenching in his chest. "For a drink?"

"Aspirin ain't going to cure me, boy."

"Neither will wine."

Nick snorted. "You got the forty cents to spare?"

Ben fingered the bus fare in his pocket that Lorraine had given him. "I want something in return," he said.

Nick grinned warily. "Now you getting smart, boy. What you want from me?"

"Help me find my father."

Nick weighed the bargain. "You want a lot for forty cents."

"Then hustle for it," Ben said coldly.

They stopped in front of a market. Another wino

155

emerged, tipped a bag-covered bottle to his lips.

Nick made up his mind. "Give me the money," he said, extending a shaky hand.

Ben counted out the forty cents. A few minutes later Nick returned with his brown paper bag. He took a long swig from the bottle inside it and sat down on the sidewalk beside the market. The wine seemed to calm him a little. He wiped the sweat from his forehead and gestured for Ben to sit beside him. "Now what's this stuff about your daddy?" he said.

Ben reached into his jacket pocket and handed Nick one of the handbills. Nick studied the picture.

"He look like you," he said, handing the poster back.

"You know him?"

Nick shook his head and took another gulp from his bottle.

"You sure?"

"Yeah, I'm sure. Why should I know him?"

"Because he drinks," Ben blurted out. "Just like you."

Nick gazed at him with his watery, bloodshot eyes. "What d'you want from me, boy?"

"We made a deal," Ben insisted. "You promised to help me find him."

"Well, I can't. There ain't nothing I can do. Nobody can. Give it up, boy. Your daddy gone for good."

Ben rose angrily. "How do you know? You don't even know him!"

"Don't have to."

Ben looked down at him, sitting on the sidewalk in his filthy clothes, clutching his cheap bottle of wine. "Why should I believe anybody as pitiful as you?"

Nick stared at the paper bag he was holding. "My oldest boy be about the same age as you when I run off."

"My daddy's different," Ben said firmly. "He loves me."

Nick looked up at him. "You think I don't love my sons? Why d'you think I leave them? So they don't have to have no drunk for a father."

Ben refused to accept it. "No, my daddy's coming back. I know he is."

Nick shrugged and raised the bottle to his lips again. A few drops dribbled down his beard. Something in Ben exploded at the sight. He grabbed the bottle from Nick's hands and flung it against the wall. "He's not like you. He's not," he said fiercely.

Nick stumbled to his feet and picked up the paper bag. Wine from the broken bottle seeped through it onto his fingers. "You shouldn't be doing that, boy. You shouldn't be doing that," he repeated.

The tears in Ben's eyes blurred his vision as he rushed away. He stopped at the first corner he came to, wiped his eyes, and dumped the handbills of his father in the trash.

16

The city of broken dreams, Ben thought.

He saw it in the downcast eyes of the men and women sitting in the park with him and in the glazed faces of the people walking on the street. Not just the poor and homeless, but the shopkeepers and their customers, the weary men and women waiting at the bus stops. Lost Angeles. A city of broken-hearts.

The psalm his mother had quoted to them in the Athens had been wrong. Weeping could go on for much longer than a night.

Though Felice and Jube, even his mother, were happy to have a room at the Salvation Army, to Ben the shelter was just another reminder of their failure, further evidence of how bad off his family really was: reduced to wearing the hand-me-down clothes of strangers and having to endure bed checks every night. The cameras in the hallways, the video monitors in the lounge, the front door which locked after five, all kept warning them how much their stay at the shelter depended upon their good behavior.

And now he had broken one of the shelter's main rules by skipping his very first day of school. Ben wasn't sure what Lorraine would do when she learned of his absence, and he wasn't eager to find out. He spent most of the day sitting in the park across from the Biltmore, playing his harmonica and praying that Lorraine wouldn't throw his family out of the shelter because of him. About the time school let out in the afternoon, he walked back to the Salvation Army.

His mother and Felice were waiting in the lounge with Lorraine when he returned. From the strain in his mother's face, Ben could tell she already knew of his delinquency.

"Where were you all day?" she exclaimed.

"I went to get Millie, but I was too late. . . ."

Felice immediately burst into tears, only it was not for Millie. "Oh, please don't send us away," she begged Lorraine. "Ben just went to find my doll. . . ."

Lorraine put an arm around Felice's shoulder. "You don't have to worry. We're not going to make you leave. . . ." She looked directly at Ben. "But we can't help you very much unless we all work together. I thought you understood the rules, Ben. School every day. No exceptions."

Constance repeated the message even more emphatically when they were alone in their room. "You may not mind sleeping on the streets, but I'm not going to have your brother and sister living like that because you won't go to school. You understand?" she said sternly.

Ben didn't see that there was any choice. At the missions you had to listen to a sermon to get a bed; here you had to go to school. But who else would take his family in? Now even Harmony Camp had been destroyed. Ben watched the bulldozers raze the camp all over again that night on the evening news. Hearing the public officials and business leaders try to justify their actions made him even angrier. The camera zoomed in on a sign a store owner had put up in front of his shop: FEEL SORRY FOR THE HOMELESS? ADOPT ONE. TAKE ONE HOME WITH YOU TODAY. LET THEM USE YOUR YARD FOR A BATHROOM.

The TV story made Ben sick with rage and helplessness. That people could despise his family like that! All because his father had lost his job and left them.

Yet he knew there was nothing he could do now to bring him back.

When Constance asked him if he'd rather return to El Paso or stay in L.A., he told her it didn't matter. "Anyplace we can get a home," he said.

"Since we've come all this way, I'd like to look around here some more," she said. Since their arrival at the shelter, his mother seemed to have recovered some of her former optimism. Now, every morning, she studied the classifieds in the paper. At night, after dinner, Ben would hear her discussing jobs and apartments with the other women in the shelter.

"To get an apartment you need first and last month's rent, a cleaning deposit, *and* a job," Helen complained one evening in the lounge. "To get a job, though, you need a regular address. You put down Salvation Army on your application and they toss it in the basket the moment you step out the door."

"It's hard all right," Constance conceded. "Most people don't have any use for you if you're poor. But not everybody's like that. We've met a few good people since we've come here. There's got to be some others willing to take a chance on us."

"You find one, Connie, you got to promise to share," Helen teased her.

Constance laughed. "Well, I know this priest I can introduce you to. . . ."

Although Ben was glad to see his mother laughing for a change, he didn't see why she felt so hopeful. He hated the junior high he was forced to attend each day, and though he went to all his classes and even did some of the homework to please his mother, he made no effort to make friends there. And, like Larry, who didn't even bother to do his lessons, he never mentioned to anyone that he was living at the Salvation Army.

After school he'd come back to the shelter and sit out on the second-floor deck with his harmonica. He didn't know where the melodies he played came from, but as he sent the notes floating from the rooftop into the evening traffic, he seemed to release some of his anger and sadness with them.

One evening—a week after their arrival at the shelter—Ben became aware that Lorraine was standing on the deck listening to him. He stopped abruptly and pocketed his harmonica.

"I didn't mean to stop you," she said. "I was enjoying listening."

"I was just going in for dinner," he lied.

She glanced at her watch. "There's still a few more minutes until they start serving." She came over and sat beside him on top of the wooden picnic table. Ben gazed across the rooftop at the city's brightly lit buildings, glowing against the darkening sky.

"How did you learn to play so well?" Lorraine asked.

"I just picked it up," he said, inching his body to the edge of the table.

"You didn't take any lessons?"

"My father taught me a little." He was immediately sorry that he'd mentioned him.

"It must hurt a lot to have him gone," she said.

Ben pulled his jacket collar up around his neck, just wanting her to go away. But Lorraine didn't get the message. She leaned toward him as if waiting for something more.

"Your mother's told me how hard you've looked for him," she said.

"What good is looking for him if he doesn't want to be found?" Ben said resentfully.

"You're right," she said. "It won't bring him back."

Ben turned away. He didn't want to talk about it with her.

Lorraine rose and stood in front of him. "I've been working at this shelter for almost two years now, and in that time I've seen a lot of homeless families. In some both parents are together, but in most either the father or the mother has left. There are all kinds of reasons— divorce, death, illness, unemployment. . . .And sometimes no one knows exactly why. Like your father, people just walk out on their families. But there's one thing I do know for sure. In all the time I've worked here, in all the families I've seen, I've never found one when it's been the children's fault. Never."

Tears stung Ben's eyes. He lowered his head to keep Lorraine from seeing them.

"Unfortunately," Lorraine went on, "children can't do much to change homelessness, either. That's one of the hard parts of being a kid. Not being able to solve your parents' problems. I know how much you want to help your mother, Ben, but what can you really do to make things better?"

The question caught him by surprise. "I—I don't know," he stammered.

"Well, is there anything you can do to find her a job?"

He knew there wasn't.

"How about a house?" Lorraine asked.

He couldn't do anything about that, either. The only plan he'd ever had was to find his father, and all that had accomplished was to land them in the streets. "I guess I can't do anything," he finally said.

"Well, that's not exactly true," Lorraine said. "You can't find her a job or a house, but you can give her your love and support. It's important to let her know that you believe in her. You know your mother's a strong woman, don't you?"

Ben nodded. Despite everything that had happened to him, he knew how fiercely his mother had fought to keep their family together.

"I have great confidence in her, too," Lorraine said, "and I know she's going to be able to make things work in L.A. But that's her job, not yours. Being homeless is not your fault, Ben, and it's not a problem you can fix. You understand that?" She shook his knee to make sure that he was listening.

He nodded again, afraid his voice would break if he tried to speak.

"All right," she said. "Now let's go see what there is to eat."

On Friday night, after dinner, the residents of the shelter held a small party in the lounge to celebrate the departure the next day of two families. One mother had a four-year-old girl; the other, a boy Jube's age. The two women had become friends at the Salvation Army and had decided to get an apartment together. The welfare money they had saved in their six weeks at the shelter was enough to rent an apartment big enough for all of them.

The cook had baked a Good Luck cake for the departing families, which everybody shared. The women were both excited and a little shy about their good fortune. Ben suspected that they felt embarrassed that they had succeeded where the others hadn't. A few of the residents, like Larry, went back to their rooms rather than join the celebration. But most of the people, including Ben's mother, seemed genuinely happy for the women and encouraged by what they had accomplished.

"You've set a real good example," Constance said to one of the women. "It's a big lift for all of us to see what you've done."

"I'm sure your turn will come soon," the woman said warmly.

"I'm working on it," Constance said with confidence. "I surely am."

Later, as they got ready for bed, Constance was still in good spirits from the party. "I've been thinking that maybe we could have a picnic tomorrow," she said, brushing Felice's hair.

"Is that okay to do?" Felice asked nervously.

"There's no school Saturday. Lorraine says it's fine if we take a bus out to the beach."

"The beach!" Felice said excitedly.

Constance smiled. "Since we've come all this way to California, I thought it was time we went and saw the ocean."

The next morning, after breakfast, they made some sandwiches for lunch and then walked several blocks from the shelter and caught a bus to Venice. An hour later the bus dropped them a few streets from the ocean. Ben took a deep breath as he stepped outside. The air was as crisp as a salt cracker.

They half walked, half ran to the water. The day was cool and bright, the beachfront walk crowded with people out for a spring stroll. There were skateboarders and bicyclists and young and old people holding hands. Though the air was nippy, men and women in bathing suits sunned themselves on the beach.

"I want to go in," Jube clamored. "I want to get my feet wet."

They all threw off their shoes and socks and rolled their pants up to their knees. Even Constance waded into the water with them. They curled their toes in the wet sand bottom and let the waves wash over their legs and the salt-spray wet their arms and faces.

Afterward Ben sat on the beach with his mother while Felice and Jube played in the sand. He watched the runners jog by them on the beach, the dogs cavorting in the surf, the little kids shrieking with delight at the waves. Then he saw an old man in shapeless clothes rise and shake the sand from the blanket in which he'd been sleeping.

Maybe all this time we've been looking for my father in the wrong place, he thought. We should have searched here in Venice, not downtown. Then he caught himself, remembering the truth. His father had run out on them. Wherever he was now, he wasn't coming back.

Perhaps his mother was thinking the same thing, for she suddenly put her arms around him and hugged him. "You know we've come through an awful lot," she said. "I couldn't have done it without you."

Ben felt his cheeks flush. "I didn't do anything," he said.

"You didn't give up," she said. "You didn't lose hope. Life drains people so that sometimes they just give up."

Ben thought of Nick, and all the other broken men of skid row. "I guess Daddy was too ashamed to stay with us," he said.

"Hard times is a shame for everyone," Constance said. "Nobody wants to be as poor as dirt."

"Do you know what kind of job you're going to get?" he asked.

"Not yet," she said. "I got all kinds of ideas, though. Once we get settled, I might even go back to school someday, learn to make something more of myself."

"I think you're pretty great now," Ben said.

"C'mon. Help us," Jube interrupted, tugging on Ben's arm. "We're making a castle."

"You, too, Momma," Felice called. "We want to build a really big one."

"The biggest castle in the world." Jube threw his arms in the air in excitement.

"That's going to be pretty big." Constance laughed.

"Well, don't just sit there. Help us," Felice said.

Ben and Constance knelt in the sand with them and began adding to the mounds and turrets they had

166

already formed. Before long the castle began to spread out across the sand like a tiny city.

Jube stood up and surveyed their handiwork. "Bigger," he urged. "We've got to make it bigger, so everybody can come inside."

AFTERWORD

Although the Gibsons are a fictional family, their story represents the experiences of a growing number of people in this country. Not since the Great Depression have so many homeless poor slept in the streets of our cities.

Their exact number is difficult to calculate—homeless people are understandably reluctant to come forward to identify themselves—but experts agree that the homeless in America are increasing at an alarming rate and that their population has changed dramatically in the last two decades.

Homeless alcoholics have been a presence on skid row for many years. The 1970s saw an increase in the number of psychiatrically disabled homeless and veterans on the streets. (It is estimated that in many America cities today, veterans, mainly from Vietnam, make up almost 50 percent of all homeless men.) The 1980s saw the addition to this population of yet another group: families with children. Today the fastest-growing segment of the homeless is children. As I write this, there are nearly half a million children like Ben Gibson in America, living on the streets, in welfare hotels, or emergency shelters.

This novel has been based on extensive research, and I could not have written it without the help of a great many people and organizations. Para Los Niños, People for Progress, and the Salvation Army's Zahn Memorial Center in Los Angeles opened their doors to me. John Dillon of the Chrysalis Center and Kay Young McChesney shared their considerable insights about poverty and homelessness. Early in this project Susan Gallin and Tom Robertson offered me invaluable support and guidance. Later Zoltan Gross, my wife, Susan, and my editor, Sharon Steinhoff, provided me the criticism, prodding, and encouragement to see this story and its characters more clearly.

Finally, I want to express my deep appreciation to the many homeless families who were willing to share with me the pain of their fierce struggle for the survival. Sadly, for most of the families I met, the struggle still goes on.

AFTERWORD TO THE NEW EDITION

Today Los Angeles's skid row appears much as it did when I first started researching this book fifteen years ago. Walk a few blocks south and east of City Hall and you feel as if you're entering a Third World country. Plastic lean-tos and cardboard hovels line the garbage-strewn streets. Squatters sit outside their tents or makeshift shelters passing a bottle back and forth in a paper bag. On a recent afternoon a rail-thin woman sat on a crate smoking, shielding herself from the sun with a tattered umbrella. The shadow of her bare foot drifted back and forth across the upturned face of a man who was asleep or passed out on the pavement in front of her. Around the corner, men, women, and a few small children were already lining up for that night's bed and meal at the Union Rescue Mission.

171

Yet as I talked to the people waiting for shelter and to their advocates in the social service agencies, I discovered that, in fact, much has changed since I wrote *Come the Morning,* and almost all those changes are to the detriment of the people who dwell on these mean streets.

Los Angeles has arguably the largest homeless population in the nation. For more than a century the fifty-block area of Central City East has been a magnet for the poor and marginalized. Because it is adjacent to the railroad station and Los Angeles is the end of the line in the West, it has been the natural destination for vagrants on the move from points west of the Mississippi. To accommodate what began largely as a population of single men, a number of cheap, "single-room occupancy" hotels were built with small rooms and communal baths. Bars and brothels naturally followed, along with missions devoted to saving the souls of the men who had lost theirs to drink and women.

During the Great Depression, many of the unemployed who came west looking for jobs ended up here when they failed to find their "pot of gold at the end of the rainbow." World War II brought more single men to the area to work in the war industries or to be shipped off to the Pacific. More bars sprang up—the USO was located in skid row during the war—and more social service organizations moved in to meet the needs of the alcohol addicted. After the war, the economic health of the area's residents deteriorated even more. Transient workers gave way to the long-term unemployed and permanently impaired. The 1970s saw an increase in the number of psychiatrically disabled homeless and veterans (particularly Vietnam veterans).

In the late 1980s, when I started researching this book, a new group began appearing on skid row: families with children. They were the fastest-growing segment of the homeless, and their numbers are still increasing. In a 2001 survey of twenty-seven American cities, the U.S. Conference of Mayors found that families made up 40 percent of the homeless population. As I write this, between 900,000 and 1.4 million children like Ben Gibson are homeless for some period of time every year in America. And the problem is only intensifying. A December 2002 survey by the U.S. Conference of Mayors reported that requests for emergency food and shelter had increased an average of 19 percent in the previous year, the steepest rise in a decade.

Today in America, education and employment no longer preclude homelessness. Welfare reform in 1996 moved many more people into the labor force, but for the most part it did not end their poverty. A 2003 study commissioned by the Los Angeles County Board of Supervisors revealed that 78 percent of current and former welfare recipients who had found work in the previous five years still earned incomes below the poverty threshold. The meager earnings of most of the working poor do not make them self-sufficient or allow them to find a decent place to live. In the past twenty years the combination of rising rental costs and declining wages has put housing out of reach for more and more workers. In every state today, an income above minimum wage is required to afford a one- or two-bedroom apartment at fair market rent. As waiting lists for subsidized housing grow, people are forced to live longer in shelters or inadequate housing. In the mid-1990s in New York, families stayed in a shelter an average of five months before moving on to permanent housing. Today the average stay is nearly a year.

In Los Angeles, space and tolerance for the homeless is also shrinking. One of the recent changes in Central City East downtown has been the emergence of the toy, electronics, and artificial flower industries. Ten years ago none of these small family businesses existed in the neighborhood, but now they are competing for space with welfare hotels and shelters. The business owners have pressured police to clear the squatters and home-less from the sidewalks and empty lots. The drive to clean up skid row has led to a proposed Los Angeles City Council ordinance that would make it a crime to sleep on the streets. A wave of other California cities, includ-ing Santa Monica, already passed similar laws. But crim-inalizing homelessness will not solve the problem. It is estimated that on any given night, up to 84,000 men, women, and children are homeless in Los Angeles County. The 331 homeless shelters in the county pro-vide only 13,632 beds. There is not enough jail space in the area to incarcerate the rest.

What all this unfortunately points to is the increasing difficulty of being poor in America. Although the total number of poor has decreased somewhat in recent years, the number living in *extreme* poverty has grown. These are families like the Gibsons, struggling to survive on incomes less than half the poverty level. Desperate to stay off the streets, they are vulnerable to all kinds of exploitation. Unscrupulous Los Angeles landlords have taken over decrepit motels in crime-ridden neighborhoods and rent out the rooms—often two families to a room—for $300 to $500 a month.

Changes in the federal welfare system, as well as the budget deficits most states are currently facing, have encouraged welfare agencies to reduce their caseloads. In California this has resulted in a large increase in the number of people who have lost benefits for missing an appointment or failing to fill out the right paperwork. A 2003 survey of CalWORKS monthly welfare to work reports revealed that the number of people who had been dropped from welfare because of punitive sanctions was more than eight times as great as those who had left because they had found jobs.

Finally, the tragic events of September 11, 2001, and the sagging U.S. economy have affected the priorities and concerns of many Americans. The succession of crises we have experienced has created what might be termed a "compassion fatigue" in our country. We have become accustomed to seeing people sleeping in doorways and panhandling in the street. Concerned with our own safety and our own troubles, we find it easy to ignore them and to justify our indifference by believing that their problems are their own fault. We do not yet recognize homelessness for the national crisis that it is.

If there is any hope for optimism, it is in the dedication and commitment of the people and organizations working to eliminate homelessness in America. Many of them helped me in the research and writing of this book. Para Los Ninos, People for Progress, and the Salvation Army's Zahn Memorial Center in Los Angeles opened their doors to me. John Dillon of the Chrysalis Center and Kay Young McChesney shared their considerable insights about poverty and homelessness. Early in this project Susan Gallin and Tom Robertson offered me invaluable support and guidance. Later, Zoltan Gross; my wife, Susan; and my editor, Sharon Steinhoff, provided me with the criticism, prodding and encouragement to see this story and its characters more clearly. Paul Tepper of the Institute for the Study of Homelessness and Poverty at the Weingart Center and Nancy Berlin of the Los Angeles Coalition to End Hunger and Homelessness assisted me in updating this afterword. I also want to thank Elizabeth Goodenough for her continuing advocacy for this novel and Dean Elizabeth Daley of the School of Cinema-Television at the University of Southern California for her generous support for the photographs that enrich this edition. Marissa Roth's sensitivity, her compassion, and her penetrating eye illuminate the bleak streets and broken lives she has captured here.

Finally, I want to express my deep appreciation to the homeless families who shared with me their fierce struggle for survival. In representing their experiences, I hope I have been faithful to their trust, their candor, and their humanity.

JULY 2004

AUTHOR'S COMMENTARY

In Los Angeles, cars and shopping carts are the wheels of the poor. Latino immigrants use them to carry the oranges and cherries they sell at freeway ramps. Tattered tramps steer them from one trash barrel to another in the parks as they root for cans and bottles to recycle for cash. Barefoot men also wheel them on the sidewalks downtown, and at the beaches in Venice and Santa Monica, filled with dirt-caked blankets and grimy sleeping bags and, occasionally, a tiny American flag fluttering in the breeze.

In the late 1980s, as I drove to work each day at the University of Southern California, I began to notice more and more women pushing these carts. Often trailing behind them were children. Wherever I drove in the city, I saw forlorn-looking families huddled in the doorways of skid row shops, standing on food lines at the downtown missions, camping under freeway underpasses. Something was clearly changing in America.

Twenty years earlier I had made a documentary film about Peace Corps volunteers working in a rural village in Colombia about fifty miles outside Bogotá. Every time I went into the city, I was astonished at the thousands of children who lived in the streets of Colombia's capital—gamins sleeping in doorways, under bridges, even in sewers, often wearing more dirt than clothes. Most of these children were seven to fourteen years old. They were orphaned, or abandoned, or they had run away from home to escape their parents' brutality or grinding poverty. They survived by begging, stealing, and selling their bodies.

Growing up in a repressed, upper-middle-class family, I'd often fantasized about running away from home as a child. Discovering children who had actually lived my fantasy, I was both fascinated and appalled, attracted by the boldness with which they accosted me for pesos, but also frightened by their reputation for thievery. In the end, my wariness and rudimentary Spanish kept me at a distance.

Over the years I continued to think of the gamins, but they were far away in Bogotá and I was involved in other projects. Now, suddenly, poor children were sleeping on the streets of Los Angeles. I no longer had to travel to another continent, or speak another language, to talk to them.

Despite my privileged background, I'd had some previous experience with poverty. In the late 1960s I'd made *Huelga!*, a documentary about Cesar Chavez and the struggle of migrant farmworkers to form a union in the grape fields of California. I had also produced *The Foreigners* for the Peace Corps, a film about idealistic young Americans trying to improve the impoverished lives of the campesinos living in the Colombian Andes. As an undergraduate at Harvard, I had also worked a summer as a youth counselor in Tanzania. But even though I had lived and worked among the poor for several months at a time, I was always aware that, at any moment, I could return to the comfort and security to which I was accustomed.

I am hardly the first documentarian to note that contradiction. There is a long tradition of middle-class intellectuals making field trips to observe the destitute and dispossessed. In 1936, George Orwell (Eton) went to Lancashire and Yorkshire to see "the English working class at close quarters" and "what mass-unemployment is like at its worst." The summer of the same year, writer James Agee (Harvard) and photographer Walker Evans (Yale) journeyed to Alabama for *Fortune* magazine to document "the daily living and environment of an average white family of tenant farmers." The year before, filmmakers Edgar Anstey and Arthur Elton (Cambridge) took their movie cameras to the slums of East London to expose the shameful housing conditions of the working poor. The results of their investigations— *The Road to Wigan Pier, Let Us Now Praise Famous Men,* and *Housing Problems*—reflect the conflicts inherent in all such encounters.

Barriers of class, income, and power are not easy to overcome. The twin dangers of patronizing or romanticizing the poor are always present. In the 1930s in Britain, a group of Oxford- and Cambridge-educated socialists, led by John Grierson, had the revolutionary goal of putting the "real" working man on the screen. Until then, working-class characters in British movies were comic figures or objects of derision. Grierson and his colleagues would show the world the true life of the laboring class. But within a few short years the "worker-as-hero" had shifted to "worker-as-victim," exemplified by Anstey and Elton's 1935 *Housing Problems*. The worker-as-victim tradition of the Griersonian documentary persists to this day. Well-intentioned social reformers continue to stick their cameras and microphones in their subjects' faces, urging them to tell us how miserable, how wretched they are. All too often, society's victims become the media's victims as well.

Orwell and Agee never patronized their subjects, but both sometimes exalted and glorified them. It was not just humbling but "humiliating" for Orwell to watch the coal miners toil deep within the earth: "It raises in you a momentary doubt about your own status as an 'intellectual' and a superior person generally. For it brought home to you, at least while you are watching, that it is only because miners sweat their guts out that superior persons can remain superior."

Agee, with his incantatory prose and evocative lyricism, wrote reverentially, even worshipfully, about the central Alabama sharecroppers. At the same time, he constantly agonized about his own "adequacy" for the task of accurately describing his subjects. His tortured, anguished book alternates between ennobling the tenant farmers for having survived the poverty into which they were born and raging at their stunted, crippled lives, "cheated and choked" of opportunities.

I had read both these books and seen the films made by the British documentarians in the 1930s. I thought I knew the pitfalls involved. But knowing the problems others have encountered does not necessarily mean you can avoid them yourself. Uncertain how to begin my research, I decided a good first step would be to observe the homeless where they gathered. In an effort to appear inconspicuous, I donned my garden clothes— dirty jeans, a ragged shirt, torn tennis shoes—and drove downtown to San Pedro and Sixth. I loitered less than ten minutes on the corner before men in clothes much stiffer with dirt than mine begin hitting me up for money. I asked one man what gave me away. "Your glasses," he pointed out, "your trimmed beard. And you don't smell like you've been living on the streets."

Driving back to the safety of my home, I thought of Orwell's diatribe in *The Road to Wigan Pier* about "the real secret of class distinctions in the West. . . . It is summed up in four frightful words which people nowadays are chary of uttering, but which were bandied about quite freely in my childhood. The words were: *The lower classes smell.*" Now here a similar charge was being made against me. I didn't smell right. I had been sniffed out as an impostor, a spy. No disguise could hide the fact: I smelled distinctly middle class and foreign.

I promptly gave up my inept attempts at camouflage and decided to present myself as the writer/filmmaker I was. For the next few months, several nights a week at dinnertime, I visited downtown shelters and announced that I was researching homelessness—I hadn't yet decided whether I was going to write a book or make a film—and invited people to talk to me about their experiences. At first the families were a little wary, but as I became a familiar presence at the shelters more people began to seek me out. After many years as a filmmaker, I've come to realize that people talk to you not just because you are a sympathetic listener but because they need to tell their stories. Telling your story is a way of making sense of your life, and many of the adults and children who sat down to talk to me at those shelters badly needed to understand how they'd arrived there. How, in the richest country in the world, had they been cast out into the streets?

Night after night I filled my notebooks with heartbreaking stories—eviction, unemployment, illness, addiction, desertion—pain upon pain. Returning week after week, seeing the same families over time, I began to appreciate the multiple dimensions of homelessness. While lack of affordable housing is the primary cause of homelessness in America, people who end up sleeping in public shelters generally have several problems. They often lack education. They've been in trouble with the police. The women have been abused by their husbands and, in turn, sometimes abuse their children. Some are victims of mental illness; others suffer from drug and alcohol addiction. Without decent, stable housing, families have trouble managing their daily lives. Children are more likely to drop out of school and engage in antisocial behavior, and their health and safety suffer. These problems compound and aggravate one another to create a pattern of despair and defeat that is difficult to break. Twenty-five to thirty years ago, when more low-income housing was available, poor families with these kinds of problems might not have ended up on the doorsteps of emergency shelters, but most cities no longer have enough beds to accommodate the people who line up for them each night.

Whatever the circumstances that reduced these families to their present helplessness, there were two traits they almost all shared. One was a continual and pervasive sense of fear. It's not just the middle class who fear the world of the inner-city slums. The people forced to reside there live in constant apprehension. Unpredictable violence—the desperation that erupts in sudden rage—affects all who encounter it. The people who live in welfare hotels, "cardboard condos," and abandoned buildings of the city face it every day of their lives.

Yet, alongside fear, many of the homeless also share an opposite trait: a strong sense of hope. I was struck by how often this hope springs from a religious faith. Many found in their religious beliefs a strength and courage that enabled them to survive the degradation and dehumanization of life on the streets. It's a faith in God independent of established religion and churches, because the churches, like the rest of our society, have often locked their doors against or ignored the homeless, or in some cases, have even exploited the poor for their own self-aggrandizement. Homelessness has a way of bringing out both the best and worst in people, encouraging both generosity and callousness, charity and prejudice.

Finally, though, what struck me most forcibly about the homeless families I met was the bewilderment and helplessness of the children. Children are not without their own courage and faith, strength and resilience.

However, not knowing where you will sleep from night to night is a paralyzing situation that makes even the most resourceful feel impotent, and children, in particular can do little to alter their circumstances. Poverty and homelessness are not problems created by children. They are problems created by adults and by our political system and its priorities—priorities that make it easier to wage war in Iraq than to wage war against poverty at home—yet every day children are forced to live with the consequences of these problems. Talking with them, I shared their frustrations and their outrage at the injustice of their situation.

First, you try to see clearly; then you try to render a faithful account of what you've seen and experienced. Since I write books as well as make documentary films, I have a choice of media. There are always financial considerations, of course. You can't make a film without money—although digital cameras are now making it much more possible to do so on a shoestring—but there are other important issues as well. What is the best medium to communicate the story? What audience are you trying to reach? To me the critical question in regard to homelessness was my relationship to my informants.

Agee begins his book, *Let Us Now Praise Famous Men,* on tenant farmers with this preamble: "It seems to me curious, not to say obscene and thoroughly terrifying, that it could occur to an association of human beings drawn together through need and chance and for profit into a company, an organ of journalism, to pry intimately into the lives of an undefended and appallingly damaged group of human beings, an ignorant and help-less rural family, for the purpose of parading the naked-ness, disadvantage and humiliation of these lives before another group of human beings, in the name of. . . ." Then he goes on to cite a long list of suspect justifica-tions for such an effort. Hundreds of pages later, as he comes to the close of his tormented book, he is certain he has betrayed the poor lives of his subjects: "I dread to dare that I shall ever look into your dear eyes again," he rues.

In her famous book *The Journalist and the Murderer,* first published in its entirety in the *New Yorker,* Janet Malcolm contends that all journalists know that what they do is "morally indefensible," that they prey on "people's vanity, ignorance, or loneliness" and inevitably betray their trust—"without remorse," she emphasizes. However, like Agee, most journalists and documentary filmmakers I know worry about their effect on their sub-jects' lives. Agee changed the names of the tenant fami-lies he described to preserve their anonymity and avoid subjecting them to public scrutiny (although Evans's photographs clearly revealed who they were). While *Let Us Now Praise Famous Men* sold only 600 copies when it was first published in 1941, the enormous exposure of film and television makes the risk of shame and embar-rassment even greater today. In *Housing Problems,* Edgar Anstey filmed a woman who broke her broom trying to kill a rat. When he took her to see the finished movie at a West End theater, she was shocked. She had never seen a photograph of herself before and couldn't believe she was the person magnified on the screen. As primi-tive people intuitively recognize, but most of us who live in the digital age would like to deny, the camera can be a stealer of souls—a curse, an evil eye. Once your photograph has been taken, the image no longer belongs to you but to the filmmaker who has captured it.

As the woman in *Housing Problems* discovered, watching yourself onscreen along with an audience of strangers can be extremely discomfiting. Who knows how they will perceive or judge you? Today, in America, there is a stigma associated with being homeless, a burden of shame and failure. It is one thing to confess your troubles to a sympathetic listener whose response you can observe but another to broadcast them to millions of unseen viewers who may be watching with very different eyes. The majority of families I interviewed were not eager to appear on television.

The shelters where I did my research were the best in the city. Although they could only accommodate a few families, the staff worked hard to connect their residents to jobs and housing and to social services that could help them get back on their feet. Many of the people I talked to were nearing the end of their ordeal. They wanted to put their past failures behind them. They wanted to spare their children any more humiliation and pain.

Since seeing children living on the streets first drew me to the subject of homelessness, I understood and respected their parents' feelings. The more I thought about it, the stronger I felt that a novel would be a better way to communicate what I'd learned. In a work of fiction, I would be able to draw from all my interviews by creating composite characters. I could be faithful to what I'd heard and witnessed and still protect the identity of my informants.

There was still one experience I felt was necessary to write a realistic account of homelessness: spending a few nights in a welfare hotel. I packed a few possessions in an old duffle bag and went downtown to find a suitable place. The desk clerk showed me around the hotel. It was as filthy, as nauseating, as I'd been told. I thought perhaps I could find a better one. I went to a second hotel. The manager led me up the rotting steps to a vacant room on the third floor. When he opened the door, a rat scurried across the floor. "Was that a rat?" I asked. "I didn't see nothing," he replied. I tried one more hotel. The stench in the lobby was enough to drive me outside.

I asked myself: Do I really need to stay overnight in these welfare hotels to know how terrible they are? Agee had an epiphany during a sleepless night he spent battling lice and fleas in the bedding of a tenant family he visited. I had mine on the street outside that skid row hotel. I knew I had come to the end of my research. I went home and started writing that weekend.

Come the Morning was a difficult book to write. I didn't want to minimize the grim realities I had observed, and I didn't want to reduce my characters to helpless victims. I wanted to convey both the suffering and the resilience of the families I had interviewed, without romanticizing or sentimentalizing them. Most difficult of all was finding the right ending for the book—one that offered some hope to my fictional family in a way that didn't distort or misrepresent the experience of the majority of homeless people in this country.

Most authors who write for children are optimists at heart; consequently, most of our books have happy endings. We want to give our readers hope and encouragement that they can solve their problems. We want to believe in the future as much as they do. Still, even if children want happy endings, they resent being lied to, and they see through phoniness and dishonesty much faster than adults. More than happy endings, children want the truth.

Despite parents' efforts to shield them, children are also very sensitive to issues of money. In our consumer-driven society they're conscious of brand labels, the prices of clothes and toys, and what their parents can or can't afford. Even if they come from affluent families, they have usually been exposed to poverty in some way, know families who have suffered economic hardships, or have seen homeless people on the streets or television. They've also observed their own parents' insecurities about money. Whatever their economic circumstances, money is something they worry about.

Poor children want to understand how others in similar circumstances cope with their feelings of anger, deprivation, and envy. Middle-class children wonder if they should fear the poor or pity them, and what might happen if their own family's fortunes were to founder. They also wonder how to help.

From discussions I've had with children, I've discovered that not all of them find the ending to *Come the Morning* satisfying. When they object, I ask them how they would have concluded the story. Some propose a traditional fairy-tale ending—the return of the father, for example, with a new, high-paying job—but this idea is usually promptly challenged by their more realistic or skeptical peers. Others respond with innovative solutions to the problems presented in the book—like Constance appearing on a talk-radio program and offering to work in exchange for rent. The energy and imagination they invest in finding solutions to the Gibsons' problems reinforce my belief in the resilience of many children to survive even such crushing and bewildering conditions as homelessness.

Of course we all bring our own personal histories, our own odysseys of exploration, to the stories we tell. *Let Us Now Praise Famous Men* and *The Road to Wigan Pier* are as much about their writers as they are about the tenant farmers and miners with whom they lived. When we write about the poor and the marginal, we are testing our own morality and ethics, our own convictions and loyalties. Do we align ourselves with the dispossessed or with our own class and privilege? The process forces us to examine our values and to face who we are and what we stand for.

Writing *Come the Morning* was also a way to discover why the image of children sleeping in doorways has haunted me ever since I first observed them in the streets of Colombia. Perhaps it goes back even earlier to my first reading of *Oliver Twist* as a child. Although I have never slept on sidewalks or in abandoned buildings, I have a strong identification with children who do. Researching and writing this book gave me a chance to explore that identification. You may start with other people's lives, but it's always your own that you come back to.

In writing about Ben Gibson, I realized I was also writing about my own childhood feelings of alienation and injustice. Like Ben I believed that if only I could be good enough, do everything that adults asked of me, then all my problems would disappear. Of course the world doesn't operate that way, as both Ben and I discovered. I shared his anger and bitterness toward the unfairness of life. Ben's longing for his absent father, his idealization of his missing parent, reflects my own history and childhood longing for a magical solution to my problems. Although our economic circumstances as children were radically different, Ben's psychological precariousness was very familiar to me.

Dorothy Day, who for almost fifty years ministered to the poor and homeless at the Catholic Worker soup kitchen she helped found on the Lower East Side of New York, often spoke about how reaching out to others was a statement of our own need for help. Wary of the self-importance and vanity that can corrupt the caregiver—and separate them from the very people they serve—she identified much more with the hurt and jeopardy of the needy. Offering food to the hungry and shelter to the homeless, she said, reminded her daily of her own spiritual hunger, her own vulnerability and uncertainty of where she belonged in God's eyes.

The only hope we have of ending the great shame and scandal of homelessness in America is recognizing our kinship—our common humanity—with the people we see sleeping on the grates and in the gutters of almost every city in our country. I'm gratified that many children and adults have responded in this way to the struggles the Gibsons undergo in this book. After a talk to a school in Montecito, a wealthy suburb of Santa Barbara, California, a twelve-year-old girl timidly approached me. "I've always been afraid of the homeless," she said. "I'd see them on the street and cross to the other side. But after I read your book, I realized the homeless were a lot like my own family—except they didn't have money."

I hope more people can make that identification, because the number of homeless families has increased significantly in the last decade. If we continue to ignore or disdain them, we risk our own humanity as well as theirs.